Frances Gapper's short stories have appeared in various magazines and anthologies, including *Time Out* (London), *Diva* magazine and *The Diva Book of Short Stories*. She is the author of one novel for adults, *Saints and Adventurers* (Women's Press, 1988), and one for children, *Jane and the Kenilwood Occurrences* (Faber, 1979), and is working on a third.

Absent Kisses

FRANCES GAPPER

The same or different versions of some of these stories have appeared
in the following publications (many thanks to the editors):

Pretext 5, ed. Ali Smith and Julia Bell, Pen&inc;
The Penguin Book of Lesbian Short Stories, ed. Margaret Reynolds;
Reader I Murdered Him Too, ed. Helen Windrath, The Women's Press;
Wild Hearts, ed. The Wild Hearts Group, Sheba;
The Diva Book of Short Stories, ed. Helen Sandler;
Sleeping Rough, ed. Christina Dunhill et al, Lime Tree;
Diva magazine; *Time Out*.

First published 2002 by Diva Books,
an imprint of Millivres Prowler Ltd, part of the Millivres Prowler Group,
Spectrum House, 32-34 Gordon House Road, London NW5 1LP, UK

www.divamag.co.uk

A catalogue record for this book is available from the British Library

ISBN 1 873741 78 2

Printed and bound in Finland by WS Bookwell

Distributed in the UK and Europe by Airlift Book Company,
8 The Arena, Mollison Avenue,
Enfield, Middlesex EN3 7NJ
Telephone: 020 8804 0400
Distributed in North America by Consortium,
1045 Westgate Drive, St Paul, MN 55114-1065
Telephone: 1 800 283 3572
Distributed in Australia by Bulldog Books,
PO Box 300, Beaconsfield, NSW 2014

Foreword

Foreword

Frances Gapper is a doyenne of deadpan extraordinariness. She has the devil-may-care punny panache to call a giant snail Mr Shelley and at the same time the ability to make a near-tragic fable out of what happens when a woman falls for him and has to face the unlikeliness of the species of her soulmate. She has the sleight of hand to drop Philip Sidney, the Elizabethan poet, into a contemporary computer department of a place that's just been painted a horrible colour to "motivate" its staff. In these stories mermaid meets mobile phone and is fascinated by its beeps and lights, a woman finds out what it means to be loved by a lawn-mower, there's a lesbian seagull, a real life Assumption, a fairytale hits the London Underground and, incidentally, Virginia Woolf and John Donne are convincingly unmasked as vampires.

These are stories by a writer who loves language (her English is redolent with all its centuries) and loves books, a writer who's more than at home with a literary tradition – someone, in fact, who's beyond tradition, who can take it into the new and the now, who knows to rewrite Jane Eyre adding a love affair with a horse. Gapper stories carry that ingenious surprise which means something truly crafty is happening. The stories in *Absent Kisses* are a combination of modest and English and totally other, out of the ordinary, a combination that recalls Stevie Smith, yes, (one of the stories is self-announcingly Smithian) but a lot more too – Shakespeare and Hardy and the Brontës are in here, and the dream-anarchy of Leonora Carrington, and the thin sharp ghost of Charlotte Mew, and a whole rangy anarchic other-tradition of mischievous risk-taking which understands the uses, the energy and the sheer necessity of deviation of both content and form, a crucially alternative tradition which stretches from Sylvia Townsend Warner through Virginia Woolf (the vampire) to Jeanette Winterson. It's a tradition which vitally reconstitutes not just norm and expectation but the potential of living.

These stories have a fused exactness and wildness – this exact wildness, or wild exactness, this way of giving a story gravity, precision, and unexpected teeth and wings, should be called Gapperesque. Wildness is all through this book in a celebration of the untamed nature of everyday urban lives; the book is full of unexpected fish and birds and cats and slugs and wolves – wolves who, naturally, like to eat Mr Kipling cakes best. *Absent Kisses* is full of these straight-faced jokes, and sudden, unlaced dreams, and exact, perfectly calculated moments of brilliant surreality, hilarity, beauty, startling metaphysic. It is laugh-out-loud funny, quick and piercing. It is gloriously arch and rich, and excitingly clever. It is an extraordinary and wonderful read.

Ali Smith

Absent Kisses

For SH, HS

Thank you AS, LL, VGL, WW

and thanks to CMcG for the lawnmower

Contents

The Ark   1

The Lawnmower   9

but that if   21

The Assumption   29

Boating in the Park   39

Pink and Blue   45

The Flood   51

River Life   61

Hooked   71

Nora   79

Seven Swans   89

Cheese   97

Slug Heaven   103

Neighbours   113

Red Office   123

Mr Shelley   137

Lupercal   147

The Bulking Store   155

Our Sweetness and Our Hope   163

The Secret of Sorrerby Rise   183

The Ark

The Ark

The company produced trade newsletters, our flagship title was *Curtains & Blinds Bulletin*. I edited a spin-off, *Nets Week*. Gregory, the boss, would sometimes give us all a lecture or pep talk in his glass-walled office. Anything might inspire him to call us in – the last time he'd just read a book on climbing Everest by Chris Bonington. His lecture was about how through teamwork *Curtains & Blinds* could scale the peaks while not falling into the crevasses, you can imagine the sort of thing.

Only one person, Mary Murchie of the sales team, was absent that day. Next morning she tapped on Gregory's door and he greeted her cheerily. "Ah, Mary! Let me just recap on a few things I was saying to the others..."

"Gregory, I've come to resign," she said. He looked taken aback, but insisted on giving her the lecture anyway and she listened politely. When he'd finished, she handed in her notice.

I hoped to imitate Mary Murchie's quiet resolution. Meanwhile I re-read a self-help book called *Do It!* which always makes me feel better – almost as though I am really Doing It, which I'm not, of course, I'm still just thinking about it and putting it off.

"*I'll* do it," Sue said. "What's Gregory's e-mail address?"

"No I will, I will resign soon. Next week. Or in June, when I have my assessment. Yes! That'll be the ideal opportunity!"

"I don't believe you."

My body was changing, ageing. Every time I looked, some new decrepitude. I was using practically a tub of Nivea a week. My skin looked shiny and satiny in places, in others like fish-scales. Maybe I was turning into a fish? A terrible fish as in the Sylvia Plath poem, rising towards myself, but what did she know about growing old?

In the early mornings before work I would sit on the back doorstep and watch the planes. Top fish, middle fish and bottom fish, a well-balanced tankful. The skies were blue, it was spring. I could never not hear the planes and traffic.

Sue said: "I can't stay here all my life. When are we leaving?"

"Where will we go?"

"How will we..."

Each of us thought the other might know the answers. I felt responsible for Sue having fetched up in this suburban backwater, this stagnant pond. All the houses were double-glazed except ours and we were being targeted by many salespeople, but I knew double-glazing wasn't the answer. I knew that much. We were both saving hard. Next year...

A brochure arrived. Canal holidays in Britain. Pretty pictures. Maybe I should be working on a magazine about canals and barges.

The cat gave me a peculiar look, between meaningful and decadent, one eyelid drooped. Then he walked past me down the hall and waited by the back door. I opened it, he went out.

The blossom on the plum tree had turned brown, the clematis

was a mass of pink buds, next door's lilac was leaning over the
fence and its offshoots were springing up below, in our garden.
The only thing doing absolutely nothing, zilch – no leaves, no sign
of buds even – was the walnut tree. The cat lay down underneath
it.

I thought the tree might be dead, so I went to check. It wasn't.
Then I examined the cat. He was.

A fly settled on his open eye. He really was.

My mother had a ginger cat called Jeffrey. They'd been together
since before she was married. One morning when I came down to
breakfast there was Jeffrey on a chair, dead. Cold fur, a fur coat
with no life inside. Cat spirit fled. My mother thought it was good
for children to "learn about death".

One simple lesson, taught over and over again.

We wrapped Mervyn in a striped towel and Sue dug his grave
under the tree. Afterwards I showed her the brochure and suggested we go on a canal trip. She looked thwarted, baffled, for a
moment, then was politely enthusiastic. So I booked the holiday.
Abingdon to Lechlade and back in two weeks.

It rained. And rained. It rained and rained. Not in drops, in
lumps. Clotted rain. The sky was haemorrhaging. Only amphib-
ians could breathe in such a deluge. We huddled below. The roof
leaked, our bedding was soaked. Rubbing the steamed-up cabin
window I couldn't see the river bank, only swirling, roiling green-
grey water. I saw trees and furniture being carried past at tremen-
dous speed.

"We're marooned," Sue said. "Don't go out there!"

I'd already, before the storms, fallen overboard several times,
through carelessness and short sight, once in a swimming costume
and twice fully clothed, I'd lost a shoe and a pair of glasses. "Here

we go again!" I would think as the world sped past. Drowning – what I feared most apart from spiders. Rushing into me through nose, ears, mouth – then choking, streaming out of me. Life! Air!

A hush woke me in the night. It wasn't raining. Then came a thump on the cabin roof, followed by the sound of wet fur being shaken. Sue in her sleep made a little welcoming noise, as she would greet Mervyn when he jumped on our bed.

The dawn brought a lighter, more silent world than I'd ever known. It was like the beginning of time, before the land's up-heaval and God dividing the waters from the waters.

Our night visitor was a rough cat, a one-eyed bruiser. He de-voured a bowl of cornflakes with long-life milk, while Sue dived to untie the boat from a submerged tree by the vanished canal. Another cat came swimming towards us with a kitten in her mouth. Our boat had become an ark, a refuge.

Beneath the watery expanse lay fields, woods, factories, towns, houses, libraries, offices. How many people were drowned? My brother and his girls in Whitechapel, my south London brother, my sister on Hayling Island? Or maybe it was only a minor over-flow, a localised cataclysm. Life would be going on as usual else-where, perhaps. We had no way of telling. I used to read *Metro*, the free newspaper, every morning on the tube, my update on world-wide disasters – now I was actually in one, I knew nothing about it.

Some days we would just drift, to save fuel. I liked those times – it seemed better than pretending to have a purpose. A purpose-less life, I thought, is maybe the best sort. Why, now anything might happen to us. Meanwhile I absorbed the light, the shining water, it was like drinking glass after glass of white wine. Family connections gone, friends cast off. Like dying, letting it all go in one moment.

A helicopter flew past, ignoring us.

I fished, the cats ate.

I thought of my shoe, sunk in the deep ooze, its white laces drifting like fronds or tentacles. And my glasses, which I didn't need now. And my job – my job that had finally left me. I imagined Gregory swimming round and round his glass-walled office. I've heard that goldfish have extremely short memories, so they never get bored, but maybe that's just something we say to comfort ourselves.

How tired I'd been, I realised now, as we chugged northwards across the floodplain. I used to dream I was so weak, I could hardly get dressed. I would be trying to pack my suitcase, to go somewhere urgently. Then I'd wake in a panic. At the end of the day I was so tired – not in a good way, an ill exhaustion. I was afraid I might have cancer. But now I felt OK.

On the fifteenth day a huddle of spires and towers appeared on the horizon, a city or the drowned remains of one, and we set our course that way.

The Lawnmower

The Lawnmower

Mary got three job offers after finishing her horticultural course. She pretended to mull over the pros and cons of each, but really she knew she'd choose the one in Jaberystwyth, working as the head gardener and only gardener on a 300-acre estate. Something about the name Jaberystwyth attracted her, its hanging whys.

"Please be sure to bring your lawnmower," said the appointment letter.

The lawnmower was a 21st-birthday present from her parents. Having divorced when Mary was 12, they only spoke when it was absolutely necessary, eg to buy a joint lawnmower. They'd spent a long time choosing it at the B&Q Supercentre. Not the model Mary herself would have picked – a bit too flashy, with gold trimmings to its dark green casing. But still a good one. It was solar-powered. No sun ever penetrated the sitting-room of her south London flat, but then, as Mary said, she didn't need to mow the carpet.

The sky looked threatening during her taxi journey from Jaberystwyth railway station and as they drew up at the huge wrought-iron entrance gates to the estate, the storm broke. She helped the taxi driver lug her lawnmower out of the boot.

Lightning sketched options and made split-second decisions. In a storm, don't shelter under a tree or carry a lawnmower. Take a stranger's advice. The taxi driver had seemed unwilling to complete the journey between the railway station and Mr Repag's estate. Though it was impossible to make a U-turn in the narrow country lanes, at every passing point he offered to turn off the meter and make two journeys for the price of one.

"It's my first job," Mary argued.

"They have trouble keeping staff. A *lot* of trouble." He told her the joke about dining with the Borgias, which she found mildly amusing. But then he grew serious. Had Mary no brother to protect her, no father? Mary laughed, thinking how old-fashioned this sounded. Wasn't Jaberystwyth a modern university city? Had she ever needed a man's protection? Were men capable of providing such a thing?

He thrust a card at her. "Phone me whenever you're ready to come away."

By this time they'd crossed a drawbridge over a moat filled with brambles and arrived at the great double door of the castle – for a castle it was. The taxi driver knocked on Mary's behalf. He pounded on the dark wood. They waited. The doorway gave some shelter, but rain dripped from the battlements. Glancing upwards, Mary noticed some huge gargoyles with terrified or unhappy human faces.

A pager crackled from the taxi driver's shirt pocket. "Got to go! Sorry!" And he ran.

Mary touched the door. It creaked open.

Inside, the castle looked derelict. The dead air smelled of very old bananas – dry rot, Mary guessed. Split parquet, sagging boards, necrotised joints. Near the foot of a crumbling stone staircase she just missed falling through a gap several floorboards wide and heard a whisper, a breath, a sigh of disappointed expectation. The door had banged shut, yet light was coming from somewhere. She looked behind – there was the lawnmower, standing by her suitcase inside the door. It had an unobtrusive yet conscious air, like a butler or sentry. But surely she'd left it out on the porch?

A place like this should have servants, Mary thought. And maintenance people. And gardeners – a whole heap of us. But maybe whoever-it-is can't afford...

Another light appeared, faint as marsh gas. Its source was a very small electric torch.

"Who are you?" someone croaked. The watery beam moved up and down, then vanished. "Damn!"

"The battery's dead," Mary said.

"I got it from a cracker. What did you find in yours, last Christmas?"

"Some little screwdrivers."

"Ha! Useful! Where are they?"

"I didn't bring them with me. Sorry."

"Damn." He shook the torch, which came on again. By its excuse for a light, Mary saw a starved vulture-like person, wearing a suit that hadn't been washed or mended for several centuries.

"Aiee!" He threw back his head and screamed like a peacock. "All the best stuff has gone to Sotheby's. Bad luck."

"I'm not a burglar, I'm your new head gardener."

"Unless you're interested in family portraits. That's my dead mother on the wall, looking as she were alive."

"You resemble her."

"Don't be rude."

"Why are the other pictures turned round?"

"Because." He shuddered. "If you forgot the screwdrivers, what assets *can* you join to my estate?"

"Only my lawnmower."

"Aiee! What's that thing doing indoors? You'll spoil the parquet! Take it away and burn it! Or throw it down the well!"

"But Mr Repag..."

"Lord."

"In the appointment letter you said I should bring it with me."

"That tampering typewriter!" Mary heard a faint clacking. "There it goes again! Deception and deceit! Disobedience and all those other D-words! I'm surrounded by enemies, thwarted and confused! You've got to feel sorry for me!"

"Have you tried psychotherapy?"

"Yes. It didn't work." Metallic laughter came from a faraway room – the typewriter, it sounded like. "That machine doesn't love me," Lord Repag said. "Last year I bought a computer. But I never got any e-mails in my in-box. It was too depressing. I'd rather continue a bad relationship with that sit-up-and-beg joker than be electronically ostracised."

"Quite so," nodded the portrait.

"Shut up!" He turned on Mary. "Gardener, go garden! You can start by clearing the moat."

Mary staggered back over the drawbridge, with lawnmower and suitcase. It had stopped raining. The sky was clear except for one huge light-tinged cloud, trapping the sun. She felt tempted to give up. To phone a friend, a rescuer. To leave this terrible place. But to do that she'd have to ask to use Lord Repag's telephone and re-enter his frightful residence. No thank you, she thought.

Her lawnmower had no bramble-clearing attachment. Where would she find the right – or any – tools? Or a bed, or food? Or wages?

"Now this is what," a voice said. Mary looked down. A large brown rabbit was sitting by her left foot. "Hello – testing, testing? Can you hear me?"

"I can hear *something*," she replied cautiously.

"Assume it's me, then," the rabbit said, with the patient air of a rabbit accustomed to very basic attempts at interspecies communication. "I'm here to countermand Repag the reptile's orders. Whatever they were, I'll tell you not to do them. Simple, eh?" It waited. "So give me a hint – I'm not psychic."

"He told me to clear the moat of brambles."

"Well, don't. Those brambles are there for a very good reason: to be someone's home. A warren, a refuge. A place for little bunnies to live. You understand me? But hark!" The rabbit's ears quested. "The man – we'll call him a man, since that's the guise he's adopted... You're *really* a man, no?"

"A woman." The rabbit looked blank. "A doe."

"Ah! Woman, a man, a female man... I loved that film."

"You've seen *The Sound of Music*?"

"Of course. With subtitles. But shush! Here he comes."

Lord Repag hurried across the drawbridge, a struggling typewriter in his arms. Mary felt the rabbit and her lawnmower both press closer to her legs – warm fur, cool metal. Down in the moat, white scuts flashed emergency.

"Lucky you've got us to protect you," the rabbit said, a minute after Lord Repag had disappeared from view behind a clump of rhododendrons.

Touched by a stream of golden evening sunlight, the lawnmower emitted a faint hum. "Now we've been properly introduced," the rabbit said, blinking. "I'm Joe and you're Mary."

"How did you know my name?"

"It told me. That thing. It loves you," the rabbit mentioned, embarrassed. "With a pure, selfless devotion, like Sir Lancelot. Your 21st-century knight in armour... and so anyway, forget the moat. Put it 447th on your list of tasks requiring urgent attention. I'm gonna wash that moat right out of my fur..." it sang, doing a syncopated shuffle. "And send it... excuse me. The kitchen garden needs replanting and you could rebuild the walls, if you're any good at bricklaying. I remember they used to grow espaliered peaches along the south side. Oh yes, this used to be a grand estate, all right, meaning bad times for rabbits. Bad times. And yet... ah.

"The only place I wouldn't go – I really wouldn't – is the lake. Don't go swimming or even paddling. Don't try clearing the waterlilies or pruning the weeping willows. I'll just tell you this, right.

"Old Repag's mother, August – named for her mother Augusta and grandmother Augustine – was a swimmer. She trained for the all-England championships and the Olympics by doing circuits of the lake, and she swam the Channel, all greased up with rabbit fat. Ahem! Leaving that aside, she was one remarkable lady. A rocket in a box of dud fireworks, a shooting star among asteroids, a hare dancing in a field of blighted corn. To her family, of course, a shame and a disgrace. At 16 they arranged her marriage to a drivelling lack-wit of noble birth. So far, so bad.

"Now, at that time a tree fungus-eating satyr lived on the estate. Satyrs who roam around in private or indeed public woodland are mainly OK, but this satyr – tree fungus addiction, decadent

lifestyle – had its pad in the arboretum, among the monkey puz-
zles, the cork trees and the Wellingtonias.

"The satyr saw August emerge from the lake in her one-piece
Victorian swimming costume, a family heirloom, and begin
towelling her hair. He was sex-mad, like most of his kind. Unlike
rabbits. August also had a libido, which many cold waters had
failed to quench, and her fiancé was not attractive to her,
whereas the satyr looked – saturnine. She was up for it. An exhilarating chase across the grass – costume ripped down the
seams like an old J-cloth – twin boys conceived."

"Twins?" queried Mary.

"Yes, I'm coming to that. And so four weeks later she gave birth
to…"

"*Four weeks?*"

"Or whatever. Twins. She'd gone swimming in the lake to ease
the contractions. But only one bobbed to the surface: Repag. The
other wriggled away like an eel. It's still there."

"Alive?"

"Very much so. Our own loch monster. And I could tell you of
worse horrors…"

"Don't!"

"Sorry."

Lord Repag repassed. "What's he done with his typewriter?"
Mary whispered.

"Thrown it down the well. Bye for now!" The rabbit made a
skidding descent of the moat and vanished among the brambles.

Mary was left alone – yet not. She grasped her lawnmower's
rubber-covered handle and felt its strength: the sun absorbed by it,
transmuted into a different kind of power and capability. "You and
me," she said aloud. It didn't sound silly. She'd been disappointed

on first seeing the lawnmower, it shamed her to remember. She'd wanted a different model. Now here they stood, hand on handle. You can't choose who the gods send you.

Though a mobile phone might have been more useful... no, she wouldn't even think that.

The typewriter came flying back across the drawbridge. It had two little bronze wings. Finding the main doors to the castle closed, it set off on a determined circuit. A few minutes later she heard the crash and tinkle of breaking glass.

A grand estate fallen into ruin and bad management; a twin curse. The creature in the lake might have been born first, it occurred to Mary, in which case he'd be the rightful owner.

Does a water-dwelling creature have rights of human inheritance? Did she care? No. And nor did Lord Repag seem anxious to retain her services as head gardener.

She found a tent and camping equipment stowed in a hollow tree and sponsored, according to a label, by Nomad of Jaberystwyth. Over breakfast – a box of sandwiches and a bottle of fresh orange juice "donated by Marks & Spencer" – she re-read her appointment letter. Its tone was warmly enthusiastic. The estate had great potential. "We [we? The typewriter and the rabbit?] plan to open it to day visitors, with the eventual intention of bequeathing it jointly to the National Trust and the people of Jaberystwyth. I am delighted to confirm your appointment as head gardener. Hope you can join us asap. Please be sure to bring your lawnmower."

"Secnarf Repag"

Examining the signature more closely, she saw it was stamped.

*

The lake. How could she not go near it? As a first step, she must draw up a grand design for the estate – consider sight-lines and vistas, plan walks. This couldn't be done by guesswork. She needed to go everywhere. And those waterlilies should at least be identified by name and colour. She must ignore the rabbit's warning, she decided, taking out her compass.

She walked for three hours. The lake proved elusive. She caught glimpses of it, but each time she ascertained its position, it wouldn't be there. Playing hide-and-seek with a lake was an exasperating pastime.

She returned to the overgrown remains of the formal gardens. If the lake thought she'd lost interest, perhaps it would start to pursue *her* – though her degree course had not included lake psychology. Beyond the parterre gardens enclosed by yew hedges she found what might once have been a knot garden. To the south lay a wilderness. Flowering thorns, hollies, silver birches, Scots pines. It should have paths mown through it, Mary thought, as she waded in knee-high golden grass, to make it a proper wilderness, of the early 17th century type. Profusion and control.

Under a mackerel sky, charged with light energy, her lawnmower decided by itself where paths ought to be. While it zoomed around, Mary lay under an oak, dreaming of waterlilies. She hoped for robust species, with ingenious breeding capacities. *Nymphaea tuberosa* – small tubers on the rootstock break loose and swim away to establish new plants elsewhere...

She felt a change in the air and noticed a silence. Wisps of cloud rushed across the lower sky; above hung squall clouds. The ground felt damp. She was sitting on a muddy bank, by a lake. A boat, a small inflatable, floated nearby. Where was her lawnmower?

Something nuzzled into her arms. An outboard motor, with gold trimmings to its dark green casing. It yearned towards the boat, tugging her along too; waited while she clambered aboard, then slipped or jumped into a bracket in the stern. Here it nestled. It purred.

The boat moved slowly across the water. Leaning over the side, Mary picked waterlilies. Stiff-petalled, white and candy-coloured. Species she didn't recognise. They came up easily, trailing their long slimy dark roots. She pulled armfuls of them.

The sound of the outboard motor curiously resembled the lawnmower. But she didn't need to mow the lake... She rested her cheek against its warm metal casing. That sweet, narcotic smell must be the waterlilies.

Deep water. Shapes of things moving below. Creatures, monsters. Part of the lake seemed to rouse itself like a huge bat, then flew away, leaving plenty of water behind. And though it wasn't raining, the surface was pierced by thousands of tiny gulping mouths...

but that if

but that if

My father was a fisherman and died aged 39. His boat went down in a great storm. Such a death would have seemed fitting to him – *dulce et decorum est pro mare mori*. You live by the sea, you die by the sea. Afterwards my sister Lou and I lived by beachcombing and dropping bent pins in St Warna's well, to encourage further storms and shipwrecks. Our forebears were opportunists, though not often wreckers, lacking the skill and bloodthirsty resolve to set fires to mislead ships to their doom – however, the weird currents around our isles and the many hidden rocks did the work as well. *We pray thee, O Lord, not that wrecks should happen, but that if any wrecks should happen, thou wilt guide them into the Scilly Isles for the benefit of the poor inhabitants.*

It was my great-aunt, out digging for lugworms in the dawn light, who saw Admiral Sir Cloudesley Shovel wash to land – without his admiral's hat, so she could not have known him, as she later argued with the judge to no avail. The admiral's flagship, the *Association*, had been lost, together with the *Eagle* and the *Romney*, as he was returning that night in 1707 with his fleet from the siege of Toulon. He had set their course in fog, straight for the rocks –

no one daring to point out his mistake save one young seaman, a native Scillonian, whom the admiral ordered to be hung at the yard arm for insubordination. (*No sooner was his body committed to the deep than the wind began to blow and the corpse followed in the wake of the ship...*) They struck on the Gilstone rock and its cruel reefs, near the Bishop. So the admiral was in turn helped from this world of sin and sorrow by my great-aunt, she having taken a fancy to the rings on his pudgy white fingers, especially one set with a large emerald.

The sea's largesse was seldom edible. One week, two thousand pairs of training shoes; another, seventy great rolls of industrial plastic, fit only to roof henhouses. By now the 20th century was drawing to a close. Lou and I were like two split and dried cod. The island had no fresh-water springs – we collected rain and begged or stole bottled water from the General Stores down by Anneka's pier (built by Anneka Rice and her TV crew in a day. Challenge Anneka!) or from the Fraggle Rock café. I had a longing to live by a river.

One day a bee flew past my corner of vision and, following one of its ancient routes, continued over the stretch of water that divides us from Tresco, our sister island from which we drew apart, a few centuries ago.

Our paths are graven in time, God sent the bee to remind me. How should I leave this place, where even the bees keep faith?

Firethorn chugged past, crammed with tourists. A good catch: the season must be upon us. (*We pray thee, O Lord, not that the tourist industry should flourish and the cash-rich traveller be fleeced, but that if, etc*) We had nothing to sell, for our fares to the mainland. Only one hen.

I watched a Land Rover being winched on to a boat. A flock of sheep disappeared into a hold, as into a cyclops' cave. We need only move ourselves. I could swim, perhaps – at least, in my younger days I'd swum from Bryher to Samson. But Lou never learned and is now grown too spindly. She's a tamarisk bush, with the face of an aristocrat or a goat.

"Let us," she whispered, shoving that long face close to mine, "beseech the help of the gods."

"The gods?" We were chapel-goers.

"The gods on Tresco. In Valhalla!"

She meant the figureheads. The painted charmers in their carved draperies, with crowns and necklaces and girdles. The leaping gold lion, his paws held together under his chin, his white incisors, his red tongue, his blind gold eyes. Friar Tuck.

"Since St Columbus and his brother saints crossed the Irish Sea on millstones..."

"But we are not saints, nor miracle workers," I reminded her.

"Not here. Not now. But we might be."

So we crept into the gardens, through the unofficial entrance by the nursery and the compost bins. Many plants have escaped from here, aided by the locals – sedums, echiums and cacti ornament front gardens and spread along the dunes. The figureheads too, I told myself, were prisoners and longing exiles. Cramped together in their little low-roofed shed, affixed to crude stone pillars. Courage, little sisters...

I put my arms round Queen Isabella, a blowsy and a buxom lass, to break her from the rock. She was white from head to – not toe, but only her feet were missing, her long draperies chopped at the ankle. Her right hand was placed soulfully on her breast; the other rested on a blue and gold shield. She proved weighty in truth. As I lay winded and gasping, Lou took down a Puritan Maid, just a head and shoulders, with her eyes painted in (Queen Isabel's were blank like the lion's).

With the Puritan Maid in her arms, Lou began to sing. Her chirps mingled with the gathering voices of birds, our sisters, our mothers and our daughters. Why birds should be our sisters needs no explanation; why our mothers? You'd have to have known my mother and her impatient ways. Unable to bear the clichés of human speech, the stock remarks used as echo and refrain, she would often burst into song by way of ironic commentary. So we got into the same habit; a bad habit, really. I thought my mother would not die, but fly away, as she increasingly resembled a dunnock. I was wrong, she did die, and yet since in this tree-beset land I do often hear her singing.

Our daughters will sing over our coffins... well, perhaps not. Our graves, then.

Birds will always be with us, I think. But the cod, the plaice, the haddock, the mackerel, the hake, the sardine? They are being culled, slaughtered, harvested, massacred, slain. Fished. Trout may survive on farms, the tame, the artificial variety. But what of our dear trout servants? O, I'm leaping ahead of myself (the salmon).

So each clasping our ladies for buoyancy, we swam from our island home to Cornwall. The birdwatchers taking the ferry to St Mary's and going from there to St Agnes fixed on us their astonished binoculars; the helicopters buzzed low and our four heads were twice attacked by gulls. As we approached Penzance, the locals gathered on the shore. At first they supposed Isabella and Puritan to be sea goddesses – Venus in a couple of her many guises – not perceiving their obnoxious cargo, our flailing legs, until we drew close.

Our ability to traverse a width of water made us appear something other than true dames to these locals, who thought women and seawater brewed ill – let a goodwife set foot in your boat, there a leak will spring between two caulked planks; or cast a fishnet made by crafty female hands, that net will hold naught but weed and pebbles, though it appear stout-knotted and close-meshed. For women having a kindred sympathy with fish and other marine creatures, they are as like to go huggermugger with the catch as let it be hauled in.

Either saints or witches, then.

They gifted us a piece of land, a pine tree and a broken-down hovel. It was enough. Adapting to the mainland vegetation, Lou became indistinguishable from a furze bush.

O, it was dry. The rain vanished into the cracked earth. Be still, the bird sang. Imitate your sister. And so I did for a while, a decade. Then I took the bus into Penzance – they'd started a weekly service. Banks, teashops. Half-way up the main street I spot the Puritan Maid – a maid no longer it would appear, for she's pushing a pram. "You've put on weight, m'dear," I greet her – she laughs, "O, I'm expecting another."

I say coocheecoo to the child in the pram, which boggles at me. "How's Isabel?"

"Gone to London." I see Queen Isabella at that moment, straphanging in the tube – she's belly-swoll'n too, but those fine ladies and gents stick like figureheads to their seats.

That's interesting, I've gained the capability to farsee. All that sitting around must have done some good. Sitting dry, Lou would say. We're sitting dry, we two.

Which reminds me. "It's awful parched out there in the beyond," I wheedle Puritan.

"Here" – she grabs the bottle from her kid's mouth. "I expressed this. Take and sprinkle it on the ground."

"Thanks, Puritan!"

"Clare."

"Wah!" the baby cries. It has good lungs, I compliment her.

"That's from his father's side, of course."

Of course.

Well, I sprinkle the milk as directed – I say milk though it didn't look or taste milky, but surely she couldn't feed her child on seawater? – and lo, a clear-bright spring burst forth, which made a channel for itself to become a deep-flowing river. That water always did taste salt to me, but the brown trout swam there, proving it fresh. A brown trout can't abide the hint of cutlery.

I say brown – our trout were vivid green with red spots.

I dipped my hand in the still place where they hang under the water and wiggled my fingers to entice their kittlish bodies. Tossed in the air, a burst of silver drops. Change or die! So I created a new race of beings, whose descendants may still be seen in the town. Though none of their offspring became fishermen to my knowledge, one grandson opened a fish and chip shop.

My sister meanwhile died of a plague of slugs. My fault, I brought the damp. One day I saw the Lou bush was covered in the little creatures, nipping off all its green buds. A bush can't survive unremitting discouragement. It died. The twigs broke at my touch. O Louisa.

I walked on the beach at dawn. The Blessed Isles, they called my homeland, the isles of the dead. But Lou was alive there.

Should I go back, admitting my failure to create a life for myself, with only my trickster's skill to pull other lives from their native element? What could I salvage, or plunder?

It was then I saw, drifting towards me on the tide, the wreckage of my dreams.

The Assumption

The Assumption

The same week sentence was passed on Dr Harold Shipman, the police were also interviewing me. They couldn't find a body to exhume for tests, but that was the problem. There was no body. My mother had not been buried, or cremated. This was exactly what the police didn't like, what made them suspicious of dirty work on my part.

"You stand to benefit from your mother's will," the detective inspector accused me, at Hounslow police station.

"Well, of course I do!" It would be strange if my mum had left her money, what little she had, to anyone else but her four children, seeing she had no quarrel with any of us.

"Can you estimate the value of your mother's house?"

"I don't think that's..."

"Just answer the question please, Miss Coleman."

"£160,000."

The inspector gave me a level look, out of his fathomless dark eyes. He reminded me of a fox I meet sometimes on my way to work, which bites holes in rubbish bags and pulls out their innards.

"How do you know so precisely the value of your mother's house, may I ask?"

"It's in the papers." Two of the nationals and even the *Brentford Gazette*. "The mysterious disappearance of local resident Mrs Patience Coleman (72) from her £160,000 house in Grosvenor Road..."

The inspector sighed. He spoke into his tape recorder. "I am now stopping the interview at 11.30am." He snapped off the recorder. "This afternoon I will be asking you to state how your mother died" – I opened my mouth to protest – "or disappeared, leaving out no detail that could be of relevance."

I wasn't looking forward to it. But of course they were interviewing Paul too, and my sister Louise and her husband, and the Unitarians. So, no point in telling lies.

Between Christmas and New Year, my mother went down with 'flu. She rang me to postpone a lunch date. "I'm just feeling a little bit under the weather, darling..." By the time Paul found her – he's the only one of us who sees her regularly – she was barely conscious.

An answering machine at the doctor's surgery repeated "Stay in bed, drink plenty of fluids..." but after Mum had fallen down the landing stairs, trying to reach the bathroom by herself, Paul achieved the minor miracle of getting an actual doctor to perform a home visit. The doctor diagnosed pneumonia and prescribed antibiotics. My mother, in a ghostly whisper, assured him that she was feeling just fine. Although by this point she had eaten nothing for four days, she also managed to trick the doctor into saying she needn't force food down, if she didn't feel like it.

My mother was so thin, a skeleton lightly fleshed over. "I think I've lost that bit round my middle," she said proudly, as I was helping her into the bath. Paul, who once trained as a nurse, had instituted the daily bath routine. He had changed her nightie and sheets, draping clean washing over the radiators. Downstairs in Mum's sitting-room crammed with Christmas cards and decorations, he told me about her fainting in his arms, her eyes rolling up into their sockets. "I really thought she was going to die."

I watched the millennium fireworks on television. Later that night, I woke up to hear voices talking and thought my mother must have her radio on. We were alone in the house, so far as I knew. Paul was celebrating in Trafalgar Square, with a girlfriend and a bottle of champagne. A soft radiant light was coming from my mother's bedroom.

The light, the hushed talking, reminded me of being a child listening to my parents. Once at primary school our class was asked to calculate how old we'd be at the turn of the century – 43! What had I imagined my life would be like? Did I assume I would have a husband, children? Or just think how sad it would be, to be so old?

The room where I was sleeping had once been a nursery. Alphabet letters still danced in a frieze above the picture rail. She'd moved to this house after my dad died, moved from a quiet green suburb into this area of narrow streets and Victorian terraces, sheltering behind the M4 junction. Cracked pavements, litter, pushchairs. She changed her neighbours from old to young.

I fell asleep again. In the morning, I remember thinking how rosy and young she looked, propped up against her pillows. She had to sleep sitting up, to breathe. And she must have slept – I hadn't heard her coughing.

She opened her eyes and focused. "Oh hello, darling!" She seemed a bit surprised to see me.

I drew back the curtains to reveal the quiet street, the damp slate rooftops. The beginning of a new century. Here we were. All seemed reassuringly the same as usual. Her time was running out fast, but I didn't know that. She did, but then she'd only just been told and maybe she needed to mull things over.

At the end of January, Paul called me over to Mum's house for an emergency meeting.

"Is she ill again?"

"No, she's just – strange."

Above my mother's fireplace hung a print of Stanley Spencer's *Resurrection*, one of her favourite paintings. We seemed to have been plunged into a Stanley Spencer-type situation, of biblical scenes unfurling in our own world, in 1920s Cookham/21st century Brentford.

An angel had visited my mother. Not just to chat. For a reason.

"He told me, as I was saying to Paul" – my mother looked modestly embarrassed – "I'm going to be assumed into heaven, body and soul together."

"But you're not even a Catholic any more!" This from Paul, since I was just gaping at her. Several years back my mother had joined the Unitarians, saying that she could no longer believe twenty impossible things before breakfast. She also liked the poetry readings.

"Oh, I don't think that matters."

"What did the angel look like?" I asked.

"A bit like Paul."

I stared at my brother, who of all of us most resembles my father – hazel eyes, high forehead. Maybe Mum had projected this so-called angel out of her unconscious. But why now, 13 years after

Dad's death? I knew she still missed him, but the worst grieving had passed. She'd come to terms with being alone, or so I'd thought.

"He was so gentle and sweet. He asked if he could perch on the side of my bed – don't you think that was nice, to ask permission!"

"Maybe he was a burglar," Paul suggested.

"No, he was an angel," my mother insisted stubbornly. "It was obvious. He had light all round him."

I remembered the soft light coming from her bedroom. If I had gone in then, what would I have seen? Nothing, I suspected, like one of the unbelievers in the Bible – and yet I now felt strangely angel-deprived. I knew I'd always regret not having taken a peek round the door.

The angel had been at pains to reassure Mum. "Now Patience, don't be afraid," he'd said, patting the bedclothes. "There's absolutely nothing for you to worry about. Everything is going to be quite all right."

"I think he was gay," my mother said. "He didn't have an earring, but there was something in his manner... not at all like you, darling," she added quickly, for Paul is sensitive on the subject of suspected gayness.

Seeing his blank expression, I also guessed that my brother was memorising this conversation for his next stand-up comedy routine. He crouched low in my mother's worn blue armchair, his legs stuck up like a grasshopper's. "So. The Assumption," he said, cracking his knuckles. "Did you pencil in a date?"

"Yes, next Saturday. And I want to have a party. I thought I'd make meringues."

I rang Louise, who lives down in Hayling Island. "A party!" she cried above screams, barks and crashes. "Yeah, OK! Any particular reason?"

"Mum thinks... she thinks..."

"What? Put that down! Rickie, get off!"

"... that she's going to die soon."

"Oh, bless her! It must be post 'flu blues. Or she's getting paranoid in her old age!"

Mum invited all the Unitarians, to what she'd merrily dubbed her "passing-up party".

"You can't think how we all admire and love Patience," one Unitarian said to me on the Saturday. "We think that if anyone can do it, she can."

"You mean people have tried this sort of thing before?"

"Oh no, no. We're anti-miracle, as a rule."

The house was so crowded, I'd lost track of my mother amid the hubbub. Then she appeared and grasped my hand.

"Darling, I know you haven't been having an easy time lately. I wish I could take you with me."

"Oh, well. Um. It's not too bad," I said uneasily.

"You know where my will is, don't you? In a suitcase under the spare bed."

I looked down at her hand, worn and shiny from years of housework. So familiar to me. The short ridged nails, the plain gold wedding band she bought herself from a second-hand jeweller, after her old ring of squashed gold hearts just slipped off her finger.

Other people needed her attention. Louise grabbed me. "Is it true? Is she serious?" I heard panic in my sister's voice. "Can't we stop her?"

"How?"

"Somehow!"

"Well, you know Mum. Once she's set her mind to do something..."

"But this isn't like the Open University!"

I went upstairs to the bathroom. Washing my hands I glanced out of the window, down into the little courtyard garden. Snowdrops, unopened daffodils. And there was Mum. How had she managed to get away?

She was standing in a patch of afternoon sunlight, like someone waiting on a station platform, gazing into the middle distance. Her hands loosely clasped in front of her. Neat and spruce, with fresh lipstick – and I bet she'd just run a comb through her hair.

Then she looked up at the sky, past next door's huge overhanging chestnut tree. Then up she went. Not as though weightless, or exempted from the rules of gravity. No, as if drawn through the air, as if being *taken*.

Louise was screaming, "Stop her! Stop her! Don't let her get away!" Pain in my heart, left stranded here.

My small nephew was in the garden, jumping up and down, clapping his hands. "Granny Patience! Granny Patience!" And oh God, she looked down at him and smiled. Her last fond farewell glance. At him, not me.

She was a tiny dot in the sky. Then gone.

Boating in the Park

Boating in the Park

Perhaps we shall go for a walk in the park.
And then it will be time to play until dark. – Stevie Smith

"Do you think the landscape of the dead is colourless?" my cousin asked. I looked keenly at him. This was my cousin Casmilus, who goes back and forth.

"Why, Caz, that's a very peculiar question."

He took my arm and guided me through the dark wood. The hollies, the beeches, the oaks. The rain drips from the dark blades of the rhododendron leaves.

"She communicates with her daughter from beyond the grave," he was saying of Rosamond. "She is now president of a college of mediums in South Kensington, what do you think of that, eh?"

"Oh, I don't know, Caz. I think we should leave the dead alone. How tiring it must be, how uncomfortable for the poor ghosts to be called back and forced again into human pattern, like shoes that pinch, like school uniform. To make a bright tea-time chatter with Snooks the psychic."

"Or why not call Death himself?"

"Ah, you've spoken his name, which we were trying to avoid mentioning. Or at least I was."

"Prince Certain Personio," said Caz, with his dark laughing face. "Now what is this park called?"

"Scapelands. It has nine entrances, a mystic number, owing to the enlightened arrangements of Southgate Urban District Council."

"We could visit them all, going round the perimeter path," Caz suggested.

"No, that would tire me out."

We sat on a bench by the lake, near the place where it is forty feet deep, this is where old Lady Cattermole drowned herself. The Cattermole family went away before the wars and the Vanbrugh house is now a Hospital of Recovery, owned by the Priory Hospital Group. General Pinochet was laid up here with back pain – well, really they couldn't think what else to do with him, nobody could. "I'm glad your mother isn't alive to see this, dear." My aunt, though a staunch member of the Syler's Green Conservative Association, was not at all pleased to have a Dictator living nearby, no, she did not count him an asset to the neighbourhood. And Princess Diana also visited the hospital – long before Pinochet this was – in her official capacity as Princess and with kindness, speaking words of comfort to the anxious and distressed, the people with nervous breakdowns and the anorexics and those other ones who eat their food with smiling faces, then vomit afterwards in secrecy. Well, of course the poor girl was herself trapped in that same circle of Hell – or Purgatory.

Caz said: "As a boy I swam in the rough and dangerous seas off Northumberland. I am a sea person, disliking the trapped inland waters. This lake, I observe, is stagnant in places. Are not the suburbs a backwater likewise, are they not intolerable?"

He pointed to a dinghy, painted green and white, which was lifting on the small waves by the lake shore, its painter looped around a young oak. The boat's name was TT *Elysium*. Tender only to one. Tender and true...

"The Norse death ship was called *ludr*, meaning boat, coffin or cradle," he said, helping me on board. "Even in these Christian times of ours many witches, mermaids or goddess-figures appear in boats. At the midsummer festival at Douai in 1770 I saw..."

"But you were not at the midsummer festival at Douai in 1770?" Caz did not answer my question, he appeared preoccupied with the oars. "A picture of a mermaid hangs outside our local pub, the Fishmongers Arms," I hurried on to say. "Personally I am not so glad to see these relics of pre-Christianity, no, in my view they encourage mayhem and bad behaviour. The children at number 5 go hungry and dirty while their mother and the violent lodger sit drinking. These children have been taught to steal the milk from the doorsteps."

"Good God, you are joking."

"No, Caz, I am serious, yet not aggressive, and fairly cheerful, though with melancholy patches."

Our boat sped over the lake. Caz has this weedy appearance but my goodness he is stronger than he looks. He rowed with a purposeful air. I do not entirely trust Caz, though we are second cousins on my mother's side. He would not do for a lover, no indeed. He is really one of those dangerous and seductive people whom it is best to avoid. Yet this pull between us, this whirlpool-ish feeling, curiously gets stronger as I grow older.

The Egyptian geese were huddled together on the island. A long column of midges seemed to approach us like a tornado, but passed without harm. "They should be ringing the bell soon. The park closes at dusk, we had better hurry."

"But look," said Caz. He backed water until our boat stopped. Then I saw it was long past dusk, indeed it was night and all the people were gone from the park, yet I had not heard the bell.

"Look again." I looked and saw the palings had vanished and the trees, the lake now stretched to the dark horizon, to infinity. Like the salt marshes of my childhood.

I clutched the side of the boat. "Oh Caz, where are we?"

Caz, leaning forward, took my hand. "My dear girl," he said, "you have no husband or kiddies to care for and to be frank you are getting old. The thin hair, the wise eyes in the aged face – oh it is pitiful and unbecoming."

"The unbecoming of all that we've become," I murmured.

"Exactly so. Couldn't we just skip all that and go off together?"

"No, Caz, I must say no. I still have Aunt to care for. Aunt depends on me." I shivered, feeling the cold winds of eternity rushing past, the breeze raised goosepimples on my arms.

"Dying only takes a moment," Caz said in a low, winning voice.

"Ah, but it may be, you know, an awfully *long* moment." The tears came as I remembered. "Take me back, Caz."

So my cousin rows me from the shoreless seas of the afterworld, back into Scapelands Park. Which is, you may say, a lucky escape for me. It is day again, the young girls talk into their mobile phones, "Cool, call me, yeah?". My cousin leaps to land, he secures the boat and helps me up the bank.

"Why, here is my coat that I lost." Caz pulls a fine fur coat from a hole under the roots of a great oak tree. He shrinks, dwindles, and now off he runs in the likeness of a slim stoat.

Pink and Blue

Pink and Blue

The first time you visited my house, I remember how pretty you looked sitting on my sofa – your blue skin against my pink cushions. You were my first blue affair, I was your first pink person, although you'd once had a green experience. I asked you, what was green like? Fey, you said, and vain. And jealous. I wasn't any of those things, I was pink. I felt glad to be pink, excited by blue.

Twiddling open my pink Venetian blinds, I introduced you to my garden – rhododendrons Pink Pearl and Sugar Pink, roses, clematis, lilies, hibiscus, pinks. Of course, not all were in flower. You politely didn't mention the green. We conspired not to admit green's existence. But you asked me, why no fuchsia (why no future?). Because, I explained, fuchsias are rarely pure pink. More often part-red or semi-purple.

You only had a window-box, in which you grew morning glories...

Then I ushered you into my boudoir: the essence of pinkness with its valanced bed and dressing-table, its frilly pillows. You gasped – in admiration, I thought at first. Then, unforgivably, you laughed. Oh, very Barbara Cartland, you said.

I am in fact a distant cousin of that lady. Until you spoke, I'd been proud of the connection, the extra pink credentials it gave me. Now I shrank from your cold blue laughter. As my pinkness faded to the merest tinge, you looked a bit concerned. I mean, you said hastily, this room doesn't seem to entertain the possibility of being blue, of blueness.

Looking at you then, I saw as if for the first time how blue you were, how blue. Me pink, you blue. How strange you were to me, how utterly different from myself. Afraid and longing, I asked, what does blue mean.

We stared at each other. In your blue eyes, I saw oceans and eternities. In my pink ones, you saw I don't know what.

It means, you said. But then our lips touched – yours chilly, mine lipsticked – and from then on we spoke love, not philosophy.

I found making love to blue quite frightening. Parts of me disappeared into you and I wasn't sure if I'd ever get them back. Blue had hidden wet bits, pockets of slippery-slidiness, jelly or spawn. Like *Blue Planet*, which pink people weren't supposed to watch, but I had, and was dismayed by it. The lobster scenes were most unnerving, though filmed in a Welsh aquarium. I prefer my lobster cooked and served up to table.

The bed looked as though we'd squashed grapes in our rolling around, but I was fresh enough in love to find that delightful. The bedroom smelled richly purple, I myself like that unpleasant whiff of stale wine you get from bottle banks.

Pink was surprisingly warm and furry, you said. Like making love to a novelty hot-water-bottle. Although this didn't sound very romantic, I continued to snuggle against you, thinking sweet pink thoughts. How well pink and blue go together, the contrast highlighting our uniqueness, et cetera.

That night I dreamed in more than one colour.

You departed with airy grace. Pink nets twitched – pink shock! – as you walked down the street.

Blue, my family cried, we don't like blue. People like us don't associate with blue, or marry into it. There's nothing *wrong* with blue, they added, doubtfully. It's just not fashionable.

Lavender, lilac, violet, aubergine, buddleia and plum. My children, I thought.

But looking up at the sky, I heard my family whisper – blue is such a common colour. It's just everywhere!

One day, quite unthinkingly, I put some of your washing in with mine. The danger of colours bleeding, I didn't understand. Always wash colours separately, I'd never been advised. Oh my poor clothes, all streaky and blotched! Poor compromised me!

"I'm altered, too," you said. "Regrettably."

"But you've absorbed me – see, I don't show..."

"You are so self-obsessed!"

This was so not true. I worried about many things that weren't myself exactly. Coral reefs destroyed by pesticides running off the land. Factory-farmed salmon.

I loved to watch sunsets. "They kill me!" you cried. "Pink pollutes the air."

You refused to eat pink, I found the taste of blue repellent. We stopped having sex.

You called me fey and vain. You were jealous.

So we faded out of each others' lives. I took a pink china heart you'd given me and threw it against the wall. It shattered. It wasn't pink all through, of course, but white under a glaze. I felt doubt in my own heart – was I pink all through and forever? Or did I, like white, contain the possibility of being any colour?

Part 2

Black for train, bus and street, white my office uniform. On colour Fridays, held every two months for charity, I wore grey. They didn't know I'd been pink, once. I never blushed.

Part 3

Ill. Doctor's certificate. Lay in bed. Long time.

Part 4

A bee collecting pollen in my garden. Hanging upside down from or creeping inside a flower's narrow bell, it whined instead of buzzed. Ants performed huge tasks, shifting bits of twig and carrying seeds or crumbs or fellow ants, dead ones. The smells of rain, leaves, wet earth. Convalescence. Would I do or be anything ever again.

Part 5

A new outdoors love returned me to colour. Pale green lichen blew in tufts on thorn twigs or scaled mossy trunks. I felt as though you, green, had always been my leafy partner, the stalk upon which I flower. Yet so different!

We had an ex-lover in common. Blue, you said, was fey and vain. And jealous. Your emerald face inspired me to wonder. You showed me the pinkness of trees under their bark. Pink exists in nature, you said, it need not be anxiously cultivated. Pink balsam and spindleberries and the occasional pink leaf – oh look! you cried. Look!

The Flood

The Flood

I've always hated Stoke Newington, N16, a precious enclave in the London borough of Hackney. Alternative healing, psychotherapy, gift shops, an obsession with house prices, an aspiring Notting Hill. It's the people who live there, including several of my friends or ex-friends, who I really can't stand. The people who wouldn't live anywhere else, despite the area's incredibly high levels of burglary, street crime, drug dealing and Stoke Newington Police Force, ha ha, a byword for corruption. The people whose faces divide between frozen horror and polite sympathy on learning you live in Tottenham, although in fact Tottenham is just up the road, it practically *is* Stoke Newington.

I did live in Tottenham, a quiet place apart from the riots and unpretentious, until 1988, when I became a house price refugee. Unnerved by the Nigel Lawson effect – though being partnerless, his deadline for the abolition of double tax relief on mortgages didn't even apply to me – I'd grabbed a one-bedroom conversion on Downhills Park Road, a cut-through from the A10, for a bargain price, only about twice what I might have paid the previous year or the one following. Then I got a tenant to help pay the mortgage and went to live in my friend Nina's spare room, in her Victorian house in Merde Crescent, Stoke Newington, near Abney Park cemetery. On a temporary basis, or that was the understanding.

Trapped now in my least favourite place on earth, I became withdrawn. Nina's training to become a psychotherapist involved many workshops on Greek islands. One day a burglar entered the front room behind the overgrown privet hedge. "Hello!" I cried, hearing the sound of breaking glass and running downstairs. His face looked honest, or at least professional, webbed with anxiety lines. "Please go," I said and he climbed out backwards through the window.

Nina began dropping hints about me moving on. I attacked the privet hedge with giant blunt shears. Also I helped out by opening the door to her clients. They trooped past me, looking depressed. It was 1995, my seventh year of residence. Next door's overflow pipe splashed continually onto a lower roof. The former occupant had died, a fine old woman who used to piss in her back garden in the moonlight, a true native Hackney-dweller. The house, council property, had been boarded up for two years, although temporarily squatted by young people who asked Nina for permission to run a line off her electricity supply.

I heard Nina talking in the kitchen – "… how to get rid of her… friends once, but… she's become a monster!" Surely she wasn't referring to me? I knew I should challenge her to define her terms of reference, but instead I scuttled back upstairs, like Quasimodo seeking the grateful shadows, the high solitude of his belltower. A stair creaked under my foot: the voices hushed. I should leave, but the simplest actions – packing a suitcase, walking through the front door – seemed beyond my capability. I felt like the sarcastic pencilled remarks in the margins of library books ("Trash!" "Call this verisimilitude?").

Our friendship had certainly gone downhill. We hardly ever spoke. She was out every night, visiting her friends in diseased-sounding roads – Listria, Exmer, Ickburgh. I would hear her on the phone to her dinner party hosts, explaining her special diet. "No gluten darling, it swells me up. No sugar of course, or dairy. No, I don't miss them at all. I realise now that I've been poisoning myself for years. Now I feel – not just healthy, but *spiritually cleansed*. Listen, I'm quite happy with just a plate of vegetables. Lightly steamed, no butter."

Her shrieking laughter sounded forced, hysterical. She was 55 and growing her hair. Before, graceful androgyny, a sensual tomboy, now mutton dressed as mutton. Before, six-packs of beer in the fridge, now a lonely tofu packet.

Likewise isolated I lay on my narrow bed, staring at the cob-webby ceiling. I'd decorated this room, plus other bits of the house, on first moving in. Now I wondered, what alien energy had possessed me? Lying there I felt a willingness in myself, a desire. To take something. Or someone. Yet to rape a person, I mused, would be missing the point. You wouldn't get *them*, simply by forcing entrance to their physical selves. Afterwards you'd still be alone, possessing nothing of them, knowing nothing.

Nina's bedroom – the largest and best room in the house, with three sash windows and dark polished floorboards – was off-limits to me. Standing in the shadowy upstairs corridor, I caressed the brass doorknob. It seemed to turn itself in my hand.

I prowled around the room. It smelled of Nina, it *was* her. Family money, the kind of furniture you couldn't get from Ikea or MFI, Turkish silk rugs, Venetian masks, Indian puppets.

Her diary lay on a low table by the double bed. Nina's Diary, it announced in coloured letters, pasted to the cover. Read me, see what I say.

My throat seemed to swell and constrict, as something uncoiled in my chest cavity, between my breasts. At the same time I heard a little voice, sharp as a pin. Far off, yet inside my ear. Choose now. Open the box – box it said, not book – or resist temptation. Either way, remember, you're the one in control. And this moment existed, remember.

My heart beat, eyebrows itched with sweat. Alert, alert! Intruder! – my body semaphored, as though itself being attacked, broken into. I could refrain from action, be the not-doer of this thing. But in that case, who would I be? Nothing, only my vanished former self. Not possible. Alas! – my spirit cried as it fled. And then the voice spoke again, in a different tone, enquiring sweetly why not? She never said you couldn't. Anyway, what's inside? Only words. And words can't be stolen or possessed, words aren't *things*. You're not stealing, only looking. Can't hurt to look.

It felt as though permission had been granted. So, calm now, I picked up the diary. Opened it, started reading.

"Peter Eccles. Friend of M&L. Depressive, schiz. tend. Failed stand-up com, does market research. Unattached. Consider? Nina Eccles. Nina Hunt-Eccles.

"Adrian Houseman. Freelance journalist, flat (council) Holloway. Hobby exploring prehist. sites. Parents 1 Jewish, 1 German – personality conflicts? Unatt. Nina Houseman. Mrs Houseman.

"Mike Jones. Pine furniture shop, Islington. Recent girlf, split..."

But what about me, when would my name appear? I scanned through the pages. Not expecting compliments, just something, some snide remark or moan, anything. Then I happened upon a strange drawing, of a worm or snake with human features. It covered two pages. It was me. How did I know that? From the crude shading of hair upon the worm or woman's upper lip – it was true that I'd let my moustache grow, having mislaid the Immac and stopped caring. And from the bulges around its middle portion, the flabby rings of excess flesh. I hadn't realised Nina was such a good cartoonist and disliked – hated – me so much. But why a worm? The iconography was clear – lowest of the low, crawler, etc – rather unfair to worms, I felt, as well as me.

So I stood looking at the nasty evidence I'd wanted to see, I suppose, although hardly expecting such viciousness. "Is this it?" I said aloud – my audience Nina's one-eyed teddy-bear and Cabbage Patch dolls ranged along the bedspread. Then rage. Having been so long exiled, sidelined, a ghost in this house, I'd forgotten how it felt. Blood filled my cheeks, my eyes bulged. I grabbed a pen and scrawled across the worm "This is really YOU, not me". What I meant, but perhaps didn't clearly manage to say, was that Nina's cruel caricature revealed her own ugliness of spirit.

I flung the diary on the bed and stamped downstairs. How lightly I'd trod in recent years, avoiding the creaky floorboards, almost floating – how careful I'd been to spare Nina any reminder of my presence, what a pathetic, sad, non-person I'd become! Now the floorboards cried out in seeming anguish, the stairs thundered, the front door shivered its stained glass panels. I saw Nina's distorted reflection, heard her key turn in the lock. My old timid self would have slunk away, but now I stood firm to confront her.

"I've read your diary."

"You read my..." Nina's face turned an ugly colour. A Safeway plastic carrier bag slithered from her fingers. "You did what?"

"If you want me to apologise, I'm not going to. Now I know the truth. It's you that should be ashamed, not me."

"Get out!"

"I'm your tenant, not a burglar or a squatter. I've got rights. You can't just chuck me out on the street."

"Piss off!" Nina spat. "You're a parasite on my physical and psychic resources. My supervisor agrees with me."

"Parasite! You encourage parasites, you therapists. Can't do without them. Parasites are your life blood." This sounded a bit confused, so I moved on quickly. "How much do you charge, £40 an hour?"

"On the subject of money," Nina replied disdainfully, "twenty-five pounds a week is way below the market rent for this area. That's what I mean by exploitation."

"You're the landlady, you set the rent. It's not my fault if you can't assert yourself." I'd been shaking when the conversation started, but now I seemed to have pushed through some kind of fear barrier and I felt euphoric. To say what I meant or didn't mean, tell the truth or lies, to hear a voice speaking out of my mouth, unstoppable, wow!

Nina edged past me, flattening herself against the wall in an exaggerated manner, implying disgust at my weight and the amount of house space I was occupying. "Anyway," I called, over crashes and bangs from the kitchen as she threw things into cupboards, "I wouldn't stay here any longer, not if you paid me."

No reply.

My bravado fading, I started biting my nails. Then I smelled something. An unpleasant smell, like sewage or drains.

Nina emerged from the kitchen, holding a pack of tiny Yakult bottles. She looked aghast at me. "That smell... you haven't...? You can't have. I don't believe it..."

Oh, the horrible, vile imaginings of psychotherapists and houseowners. What did Nina expect and fear to see? Faeces smeared up the walls, furniture pissed on? She ran madly around the house, flinging doors open, peering inside, sniffing. Why should she attribute the as-yet-unsourced problem to me, innocent me, you might wonder? Because I'd become a monster in her fearful imagination. Just one failure to observe "personal boundaries", as Nina might say, and now anything – anything! – could be either blamed on me or attributed to my malign influence. What would she accuse me of next, murder? I was in a terribly vulnerable position. Best be off, I told myself, before she calls the police!

Nina searched every room in the house before investigating the cellar, where of course she should have looked in the first place. "Oh Christ! No!"

I slipped into the cellar behind her. It was half-way up the steps. A dark flood. Oily, viscous.

My first thought was, how wise I'd been to store my boxes in the attic. My next thought, serves her right, ha ha. My third...

Not a thought. An action.

I still can't blame myself, though I've searched my conscience. It happened almost without my knowing what I was doing. A push, followed by confused grappling and screams. The splash drenching me too. One little brass bolt on the cellar door – more decorative than practical.

Oh Nina, what went wrong between us? Remember when I first moved in, our long chats in the kitchen? Recipes, problems shared? Wasn't I a valuable friend to you? Through what crack or weak place did mistrust seep into our relationship? Was it my jealousy of that money you inherited, the little sniping remarks I couldn't help but make? When did I become in your eyes a bad, "crazy" person, while you withdrew among the good, the sane, the psychotherapeutised? How did your view of me affect my behaviour, form the person I became? Did you ever stop to think about that? Or care?

Would you be surprised to hear that I still dream about you? Last night, for instance, you drove by in a bubble car. You cruelly refused to open the door and let me in, though we were miles underwater, fathoms deep, and I had no car or breathing equipment. "I'm drowning," I mouthed at you through the windscreen, but you just laughed, as several turds floated past.

All anyone seems to know (among your legions of former friends, all the women you've intentionally lost touch with) is that you got married. I caught sight of him the other day, sawing at your privet hedge. Is he Mike, Adrian or Peter? Or some other pathetic opportunist?

Yes, I've been watching your house. I've made a temporary home for myself in the cemetery, underneath a stone angel with a broken-off arm pointing to heaven. Your house with all its white stone mouldings looks like an elaborately iced wedding cake, like the witch's house in Hansel and Gretel. A Thames Water van is often parked outside. Three times now they've drained the cellar. It keeps coming back, like pus in a wound.

Your neighbours are having problems too, the foul dark water seeping through all their party walls, the infection spreading. Soon all Merde Crescent will collapse and be sucked under, taking other terraces down with it, leaving only rubble and broken chimney pots. Until the very name of Stoke Newington vanishes from human lips and the London street map.

River Life

River Life

I know it's expected of me, indeed I expect it of myself. Wasn't that the reason I got married? To start a family. And what better time, at least what more obvious time than now, in this idyllic honeymoon place, Celandine Cottage, with the river floating past and everything so civilised: the bowls of pot-pourri, stifling central heating on a timer, boiling hot water on tap, the tiled kitchen and bathroom, flowery wallpaper and double glazing framed by elaborate curtain arrangements.

The grassy border along the riverside is neatly mown too, with benches set at intervals. However, unfortunately people do walk their dogs along here and glance in at our windows. Frank watches TV; I watch the heron and the other wildlife.

"Look at those ducklings, Frank! How many of them are there? At least eight." Our evening walk, along the riverbank below the castle.

Frank was silent for a while, then he said "fifteen".

"Fifteen! There can't be."

"Yeah. There are."

The ducklings looked like tarantula babies – a mass of fur,

creepy-crawling over the water behind Mum.

"How can she have fifteen? How could she have sat on fifteen eggs, to begin with?" I heard the note of panic in my voice.

"Lucky they all survived," Frank said.

"Lucky!"

Next morning, I saw one duckling coming down the river. It looked somehow not right – still alive, but only just, with its little head bowed. Two swans stretched out their necks until their beaks almost touched it, but then withdrew, dubiously or with distaste. Neither would deal it the killing blow, an end to suffering.

The fish leap in the river, to catch the midges. Hurling themselves between the elements. And the terns likewise plunge down into the river from a great height, to catch fish – the first time, I thought someone had thrown a brick into the water.

I read the newspaper. Another doctor had up in court, for a mercy killing. Where do you draw the line? It's difficult to know.

The wedding photos arrived this morning. The bride carried a bouquet of white roses and pink astilbes. And frothy gypsophila, baby's breath. The bride was given away by her brother. Very little left to give, really. And nothing real, no real feelings. A mass of surface detail. But isn't that how everyone feels on their wedding day? Like, I'm not really here at all. Who are these people smiling at?

"I look fat." Like a heifer squeezed into a dress. Red face, shiny nose. Red devil eyes too, in most of the photos.

"You look all right. It went off all right. There's your brother, he made a good speech."

"Did he?"

"You remember. What he said about your dad."

No, I try not to. I try not to remember the hospital and one doctor in the lift saying to another doctor "I've been on duty for 72 hours, I'm operating in my sleep". And them pushing the feeding tube up his nose, down his throat.

The plastic daffodils in the Topsy Turvy tea-room were about a quarter larger than life-size, which I found rather disturbing. No, they must have been fabric, they were frayed round the edges. I stared at them while eating my prawn sandwich with too much mayonnaise and peach-flavoured mineral water. Frank said, "Did you like the castle?"

Thinking this rather an odd question, I replied politely, "Yes. Did you?"

"It's just that – I don't know – often you seem to get tired looking round places."

I was not tired, but starting to feel sick from the mayonnaise. Meanwhile people were popping into the tea-room to buy take-away sandwiches. "So that's two salmon and one prawn?"

"No, the other way round."

I thought what safety lies in such banal exchanges. Boring is best, so far as I'm concerned. I deliberately avoid jokes, except the most mundane. If someone makes a witty or original remark in my presence, I just pretend not to have heard.

They were bitching about me at work the other week. How I got on their nerves, et cetera, the usual things. My tidy habits, my insistence on certain routines being followed correctly. I hold a senior position and they think I'm bossy. Mary-Claire said, "What that woman needs is a big shock." I thought, no, I've *had* the shock. It's you that needs one, not me.

Things seen on my honeymoon: yesterday, a mallard drake riding another drake, in a horrible violent way, pushing its head right down into the water until I thought it could easily be drowned.

A third drake was swimming round about them without interfering – maybe it was afraid, or was being a voyeur.

I was sitting on a quay by the tethered-up rowing boats, while Frank was trying to find the boatman. I threw a stone at the ducks, but it missed. Then the underneath one managed to paddle itself to the mud and squirm free, and they flew off, high over the fields, the aggressor duck still pursuing. "I saw two ducks having a fight," I told Frank, without wanting to be more specific. I felt quite embarrassed, although I suppose these things do happen in nature.

Frank had tried at the castle, but the boatman was apparently not hiring out boats that day. "That's how he runs his business," they told Frank. So there was nothing we could do.

There is also a mad swan on this river, which patrols up and down with its wings half-lifted and curled round in a threatening way, and its head down low, making it look huge but also quite unsteady in the water. When other swans come sailing along the river in couples, it attacks them. My mother would say something to the effect of "Poor thing, he's feeling lonely. If he had a wife he wouldn't behave like that". And certainly it is the mating season. That may be the key to it all.

I also see, every day, crows and seagulls dive-bombing the heron, when it's trying to catch fish. The heron shrieks in fury and tries to peck them as they fly past. But the cruel game always ends with the heron being driven off.

Witnessing all these incidents, I get an accumulating sense of *wrong*. A feeling of things being out of control, so anything might happen in the world. Is happening. I don't mention these morbid thoughts to Frank, since we are on our honeymoon.

We have lunch at The Hermitage pub – named after a cave up-river where a hermit used to live and which is now run by English

Heritage, open Wednesdays and Sundays. Frank jokes that the hermit probably spent all his time in the pub and would then truthfully be able to say "I never leave the Hermitage". I order chicken curry, which comes with rice and chips, while Frank has lasagne, with "roast" potatoes. Parboiled and then deep-fried – not exactly what I would call roast. The rice comes in a smooth high mound, topped with a slice of tomato. The landlady wears a neck brace, following a recent car accident – a white Volvo ploughed into her car, when she was going to fetch her daughter's wedding-dress.

The fog horn moans from Coquet Island. Fog rolls on the dark ploughed earth like phantom waves. Even the river is hidden now and the tall trees on the other bank are only just distinguishable from the sky. Last night we watched a programme about the dangers of driving in fog. People in the simulator thought they were doing a steady 70mph and were astonished when told they had touched 80 or 90. The programme ended by showing a simulated multiple pile-up on the motorway. In normal circumstances of course one would keep glancing at the speedometer and Frank is a very safe driver. However, we decided to stay at home today.

Which is how we come to be making love in the middle of the afternoon. This is what people are supposed to do on their honeymoon, isn't it? Stay in bed all day? Though as a matter of fact, it's the first time since we came here and we leave tomorrow. We might have set a record for *not* doing it. But it wasn't a conscious decision: I think we just forgot.

At a certain point comes that fantastic moment, like falling asleep, when I become unselfconscious – I mean my body loses its awareness of being ugly and fat. That, believe me, is the pinnacle of sexual achievement. It even stays with me for a while afterwards. Unfortunately, our lovemaking seems to have a totally different effect on Frank. Sometimes he cries, or has a fit of sneezing. This time he just lies still. I can feel the sadness rising off him, like fog off the river.

Holding my hand, he says, "You won't leave me, will you?"

"Don't be daft."

"I've been thinking, maybe we ought to go for marriage guidance counselling."

Frank initially gives the impression of being a stodgy type – unimaginative. But in fact he's full of surprises.

"We've only been married a week!"

"I'm serious, love. You hardly say a word to me and I don't have the faintest idea what's going on in your mind."

"I don't want to start a family." Said out loud, that doesn't sound exactly true.

"We don't have to."

"Anyway, I do talk," I say – remembering pouring my heart out to Frank, during our courtship. Mind you, we were sitting right under one of the pub loudspeakers. He appeared to be listening, while downing a pint, but he might not have caught much. It was all about my dad, of course.

We lay there in bed holding hands, like innocent children. Frank is more vulnerable than I am, really. We should both lose weight.

That night I dreamed I was on a merry-go-round, riding on a big golden rooster. A number of my ex-boyfriends were there too, mounted on different beasts. The merry-go-round stopped, so I got off, and then Frank and I walked hand-in-hand through the fairground, eating candyfloss. I was about to throw away the stick when Frank said, "No don't, that's the best part." So I took a bite of the stick. It was sweet and crunchy. Then we came to a Hoopla stand and Frank bought me a hoop from the stallholder. I asked, "How come we only get one ring?" and Frank replied, "It cost me a month's wages." When I threw the hoop it went over an aluminium can, which the stallholder handed me, saying, "Congratulations, you've won a can of worms." I said to Frank, "How are we going to open it? We haven't got a tin opener." Frank told me, "Don't worry," and took the can from me. In his hands it turned into a silver box, with a lid. And the dream ended, or I don't remember anything more.

Hooked

Hooked

There was a mermaid who left the sea to seduce a mobile phone salesman. This is how it happened.

Becky had never yet succeeded in tempting a man to his death. It felt a shameful failure, especially since she was now 29, in marine years. Why, her cousin Lara had drowned 16 men before her tail was fully grown! "You're too tender-hearted," other merpeople would tell Becky – and it was true, she had let several men off the hook, for various reasons.

"Swim to the Caribbean with me," her sister Karen urged. "It's so easy there. Cocktail-fuddled holidaymakers splash after you like puppy seals..."

But Becky wanted her first catch to be a real triumph, an achievement worthy of being immortalised in song and legend, not just a trick played on the naive or the unwary. She wanted to capture a willing soul, a man who, realising that he was in mortal danger, would still choose to follow her. A man who would die for her.

It was a clear windless night in early September, a perfect night for hunting. The holiday crowds were gone, but a few local mortals would still be wandering down to the beach after pub closing hours. Poking her head above water, Becky gazed shorewards, to where the lights of Brighton twinkled.

Was that a man walking down from the promenade, picking his way over the pebbles? Or was it a figment of Becky's hopeful imagination? Dipping down again she headed inland, swimming as a fish does with long undulating body movements and rapid flicks of her tail fins, holding her arms close to her sides.

She came ashore near the glittering and throbbing East Pier. It *was* a man! Becky composed herself – fluffing out her hair, which was a beautiful pale gold with only the faintest greeny tinge, and letting her top half emerge fetchingly through the foam, having first draped a few strands of seaweed over her naked breasts.

I am a great huntress, she told herself. I look fantastic and human beings find me irresistible.

"Hello!" the man said, noticing her with surprise.

So far, so good.

"Been swimming? Bit cold in there, isn't it?"

"Oh nooo…" Becky cooed enticingly. "The water's just gorgeously cool. You should feel how easy it is to slip along and be carried down – I mean away, away on the lovely foamy tide. Come for a dip with me…"

"No thanks!" But he lingered by the water's edge, regarding her with obvious appreciation. "I just came out here to make a quiet phone call, away from all the traffic," he told her.

"To make a what?"

"A phone call. On my mobile. Here, you won't have seen this model – it's fresh in from the US."

Becky took the proffered mobile phone and looked at it wonderingly. She poked one of the little buttons. It beeped.

"You're holding it upside down. Er – try not to let any water get inside."

She pushed another couple of buttons, which produced a series of beeps. A little whelk-like voice said "Hello?"

"Look at your face!" the man laughed. "Don't worry, you pressed one of the stored numbers. My mother, by the sound of it."

"Your mother? Inside this thing?" Becky said, bewildered. "She must be the size of a barnacle."

"No, she's 5ft 4in and lives in Milton Keynes."

"Who is this calling?" the little voice demanded.

The man took the phone. "Don't worry, Mum, it's only me. Rang you by mistake." He cut the voice off in mid-sentence. It seemed to Becky a very abrupt way of dismissing one's mother, however small or far away she might be.

"You're a typical blonde, aren't you?" the man asked. "A typical dizzy blonde?" He seemed pleased to have discovered this.

Becky pouted obligingly. "I've got hidden depths, though," she told him.

"I bet you have."

"Why don't you come swimming with me? Just for a little swim. We won't stray far."

"Tell you what," he said. "If you'll meet me at a restaurant tomorrow night, after the meal we'll drive to a quiet beach, just up the coast from here, and go skinny-dipping."

Karen was shocked to hear of Becky's plans. "I'll only be going ashore for one evening," Becky tried to reassure her.

"But what if he tempts you to stay on land?" her sister demanded. "What if you get tangled up in *his* net? And what's this restaurant called, anyway?"

"The Lobster Pot."

Karen's expression was eloquent, although she made no comment. Five seahorses hung like question marks in the water around her face.

"Oh Karrie," Becky pleaded, "you know how important this is to me."

Her sister turned and swam away, her dark hair billowing like a cloud of octopus ink. Then she swam back. In a simple gesture of affection she unhooked a starfish from her arm and stuck it on Becky's forehead.

"You'll need a dress," she said resignedly. "For protection and disguise. Human beings always cover themselves with draperies, to hide their ugly bodies. If you wear none, revealing your natural beauty, they'll either reject or devour you.

"Of course," she shuddered, "you'll also have to grow *legs*. I'll arrange for some mud to be fetched up."

Becky walked unsteadily into the restaurant. She had evolved legs, by plastering her tail with mud which had lain on the ocean floor since the beginning of time.

Some lobsters in a tank waved their feelers at her, signalling frantic warnings. Becky tottered in dismay and nearly fell over; a waiter grabbed her elbow.

"Sorry," she said gratefully. "I'm having a bit of trouble walking in these."

They both looked down. Becky was not wearing shoes. Her dress, made of plaited and woven seaweed, was coming unravelled around the hem. And it stank.

Luckily she was the most beautiful woman in the restaurant; the one least in need of its flattering lighting. And she was genuinely interested in mobile phones, the subject closest to her date's heart. He made money from selling these strange objects. His name was Toby.

The waiter hovered; Toby scanned the menu and blackboard. "Just seaweed for me, please," Becky said quickly, averting her eyes from the list of specials. All around was the horrible stench of cooked flesh and she could hear dying cries of agony coming from the kitchen. When a steaming baked trout was laid in front of Toby and he carefully removed its spine, Becky nearly retched. The human world was worse by far than she had expected. Still, her plate of crispy Japanese seaweed tasted quite pleasant. She sprinkled salt into her glass of wine.

"Shall we go for our swim now?" Toby leered drunkenly. Becky smiled and fluttered her eyelashes, imitating a moth that had got into the restaurant by mistake and was now dashing itself against a lightbulb. The end of the project was in sight. All the other male diners' eyes followed her as she swayed out of the restaurant and had she not been speechless with terror, she might have invited them to come for a swim, too. Was she predator now, or prey? It was difficult to remember.

The short drive along the coast in Toby's BMW was another new experience. But once in sight of the sea, she felt much calmer and more focused.

"I'm not really what I seem to be, at all," she told him. "I'm not a woman, I'm a mermaid. My sole purpose for all eternity is to tempt men into the sea and drown them. I'm without conscience, because I don't have a soul."

All this was perfectly true and not a joke, but rather than putting Toby off, it seemed to excite him. He fondled her knee. It felt strange having one. Becky persisted: "I want you to go into this with your eyes open, as my willing victim – that way, my triumph will be so much the greater."

"I'm sure looking forward to getting in the water with you," he mumbled in her ear as they staggered together down the beach.

"Well, I tried to warn you. But you wouldn't listen."

Becky discarded her dress, which was falling off anyway. Toby's phone started ringing as he was struggling out of his trousers. So Becky answered it. He tried to grab it from her, but too late.

"That was your wife."

"Yeah."

And a baby crying in the background. Becky thought of the sweet little merbabies. They need him more than I do, she thought. I don't need him at all. Why am I doing this? "I can't," she said. And shrugged off his groggy attempts at persuasion.

"You're weird!" he flung back at her. The BMW screeched off along the coast road.

Becky sank down onto a rock and gazed out to sea. Yet another failure. Heigh-ho.

Yet she did not feel dispirited. She'd learned a lot about selling, from their conversation in the restaurant – about wholesale and retail prices, and the benefits of setting up your own company, rather than being an employee.

His mobile phone glowed phosphorescent on the shingle.

If I could only find a way to make them waterproof…

Nora

Nora

I tracked Nora from Bristol, her home town, around the south coast of England, past Dorset. Then she took off for Europe with her mother and they stayed for a while in Boulogne. Her mother injured a leg, but was still able to fend for herself.

That winter, Nora journeyed south, alone, across the stormy Bay of Biscay and down the west coast of Africa, settling in a fishing port near Cape Town. She seemed to like it there, anyway she made plenty of friends. I was planning to follow her down there, but other things got in the way.

Specifically, my relationship with Igraine – Igraine Hutchinson, the painter. At that time, late 1970s, Igraine was just beginning to experiment with watercolours, and painting Sunsets and Balloons, a series that eventually featured in the *Sunday Telegraph* magazine.

We lived in a rented flat in York Crescent – one huge room with three bay windows and incredible views across Bristol to the Mendip hills. I loved that city. It's strange how you can fall in love with places. In my first year there, I walked in a dream of beauty, around the Georgian terraces of Clifton and the vertiginous tumbledown streets of Clifton Wood and Hotwells, through the winding wooded depths of the Avon Gorge, with the suspension bridge high above, miraculously spanning the gulf. All appeared painted in the softest, most delicate colours. One part of the city was called Fishponds. There was Totterdown, where the houses tottered down the hill, and Bedminster Down, which the local people called Bed-me-down.

But my relationship with Igraine. As I was saying, well, in the beginning, we communicated very little. Did I love her, I wasn't sure. It's funny how a relationship can be good sexually, but sort of fade away at the edges, where it touches everyday life. Some days, when she was painting and I was working on my research project, we could have been sitting on opposite sides of the Avon Gorge. Without the bridge.

If I'd shown the slightest interest in art, or if she'd known anything about the migration patterns of seabirds, we might have got on better. "It's incredible to me," she would say, "how you can spend all day and half the night watching a tiny dot of light move across a computer screen. Don't you get *bored*?"

"That's Nora," I would reply. "She's my primary bird. She's spearheading this whole project."

"But you can't even see her."

"Yes I can. As clearly as I see you."

"Ha!" Igraine would make these annoying noises, which I tried my best to ignore.

I could indeed see Nora, in my mind's eye, in my imagination, or rather I could see the world through her. It felt like I was flying, the landscape unfolding below me. The woods, the fields, the ranging southern coastline, the mudflats, the shining water at evening, the misty dawns. I could even see parts of the French coast, places I'd never been. As she flew further south, I would recite the names to myself, a litany – she's passing Lisbon, Casablanca, Agadir, Senegal. She's crossing the Gulf of Guinea...

"You care more for that bloody seagull than for me."

"Don't be ridiculous, Igraine."

"I believe you'd love me more if I had wings and a beak. If I was half-way across the ocean..."

"Oh, for God's sake."

Usually Igraine kept her emotions pretty well buried. I'll never understand the artistic personality. We were getting on quite well together, till she started painting those balloons.

When I first met Igraine she was an alcoholic and had been one for twenty years. I found that attractive. It meant I wouldn't be asked to cope with her emotional needs, or blamed for them. The whisky bottle would be my substitute, stand-in, alibi. On our second date, she drank orange juice and soda water. I was slightly alarmed, but assumed this was just a blip. I was proved wrong. She was serious about me, she said, and about "changing".

She was forty-seven, I was thirty. We sat in the Three Feathers Inn by the Floating Harbour, where they played jazz on Tuesday evenings, and I worried about Nora, who was then just about to hatch. My ex-lover, Caro, was the project leader and she was making things deliberately difficult for me, trying her hardest to get me moved off the nest. Poor Caro, she died soon after that in a tragic accident. While she was observing Nora's mother and her young brood, she slipped and fell from the rooftop. Luckily no harm came to the birds. Caro would have been glad to know that.

I tried to persuade Igraine not to give up alcohol completely.

"Listen," she said, "sweetheart, you're the best thing that's ever happened to me. My once-in-a-lifetime chance. I've got something to live for now. Maybe I'll even start painting again."

"Oh yes, great."

"Would you sit for me?"

"Sometime, maybe." I turned and looked straight in her eyes. They were slightly clouded and desperate. The jazz band was playing a mournful piece, the kind of music you might hear at a funeral, if jazz bands ever play at funerals. Sometimes you can see the end of a relationship before it begins. I saw our mutual future in her eyes. It looked like nothing but pain. I didn't tell her that, naturally.

"I want to live with you," she said.

"Fine." But I'll never sit for you to paint. You will not capture my soul, naked to be observed. And we'll make love in the dark.

I take credit to myself for the return of Igraine's artistic powers, for don't they say that all great art is born out of deprivation and loss? I deprived her of what she most needed, me.

Our bed was a mattress covered in a sheet. Lying awake while she slept I watched the moon freewheeling above the city, trailing streamers of clouds.

Our project group kept in touch with research centres in Europe and Africa. Soon my suspicions were confirmed. Nora had formed an attachment. Seagulls mate for life. Nora had chosen another female seagull to be her lifelong partner, her soulmate, her joy in flight.

Disaster. I was consumed by rage, grief and disappointment.

Igraine took me to the Berkeley hotel in Clifton, for lunch. She ordered a good bottle of wine and made me drink most of it. "Now, why are you so upset?"

"It means the end of the project! The end of everything!"

"Nora's happy, isn't that important to you?"

"But she'll never have eggs!"

"So what?"

"Oh, you don't understand. You've got no idea what this means."

"So, explain." Igraine placed her hand on mine.

"I've known her since she was a tiny chick. And before that. I watched her hatching, and I made sure she got enough regurgitated fish, and later on I put the ring on her leg, and I've kept track of her for two years…"

"Are you telling me you're jealous of Nora's girlfriend?"

"I'm telling you she's *mine*. My bird."

"You can't have sex with a seagull." A smile flickered across the face of a passing waiter.

"That's not the point," I said impatiently. "We still have a relationship, a bond. She can't just go off and leave me like this…"

Igraine sighed. "It's a nice day. Let's take our coffee out on the terrace."

The Berkeley hotel is built on the edge of the gorge, so I often go there to birdwatch and fantasise. Seagulls drift through the abyss, hanging on air currents. The terrace is the roof of the hotel ballroom, white concrete, studded at intervals with round metal objects like overturned saucers. These used to puzzle me at first, until I realised they were the fixtures of chandeliers, hanging below. So if you unscrewed one at the right moment you could kill someone. Or several people.

I felt deeply depressed. The coffee tasted poisonous and I wished it were. "Did I ever tell you about my aunt?"

"Your aunt who's a lesbian?" Igraine looked interested.

"She's not a lesbian," I said irritably, "She just had an affair with a woman, once. That's an entirely different thing. Well, my aunt was married for twenty years. To a BBC producer. He was my uncle."

"You don't say."

"Listen, will you. I'm telling you this story. My aunt was perfectly happy during her twenty-year marriage to my uncle. Perfectly happy, on the whole. They lived in Caledonia Square, in one of those big white houses, and had a comfortable middle-class lifestyle. Then my aunt got involved in the Women's Liberation movement and her husband started having an affair with this young girl on his production team. With red hair. And so he divorced my aunt and married this girl. And the bridal procession drove in horse-drawn carriages all the way round Caledonia Square, with my aunt watching from her sitting-room window. And she was terribly upset. She never recovered from it."

"Is she dead, then?"

"No. She's living in St Werburghs. What I'm trying to say is, there are things one never recovers from. Devastating experiences. Like being abandoned by the person you love most."

"Or the seagull?"

"Yes, exactly."

"Sally."

I looked round and she was crying. Tears fell on the wrought-iron table. She was holding on to the table with both hands, knuckles clenched, as if she might hurl it over the terrace. "Doesn't it mean anything to you. Our making love together. How we touch."

"But that's different."

"How is it different?" All the colour was gone from her lips and her face. Nearly fifty, she looked about seventeen. I could have crushed her between my hands, like an egg.

"That's sex. What I feel for Nora is..."

"Love?"

"No, don't be stupid and simplistic. It's a sort of higher bond."

Her eyes met mine. Now free of the alcoholic clouds, they were clear green. "I hate Nora," she said.

"Well, I hate your paintings."

"Fuck you, then." She got up, searching in her pocket, slammed down some money on the table and walked out – leaving me with a pile of small change and seething emotions. And a £50 note.

I stared at the note. It was green and brown, with swirling patterns and a picture of Sir Christopher Wren.

Despite the early spring sunshine, I began to feel very cold. I sensed the imminence of loss. Two years before, this would not have mattered.

I walked slowly up the steep hill from the hotel to the suspension bridge. The bridge is mainly for traffic, with narrow walkways on each side. In a high wind, it swings about. It's a suicide point, especially for students – the Samaritans have got a notice up and the council have put spikes part-way along the sides, to stop anyone falling on the main road below and damaging a car. But you can jump from the middle, into the river.

I leant on the rail. A Victorian father threw his whole family over this bridge, wife and four children. They survived.

Who needs a family? Who needs sex? I can sleep alone. I'll find somebody else.

But our bodies fit together, know each other. By touch, smell. It's like we've grown into one another's corners. The boundaries disappear sometimes and we feel like one person. I'm not sure who's lying on the bed, or walking across the room.

My eyes blurred. Nora and Igraine. I lost my bird, I lost my girlfriend.

"Sally?" A touch between my shoulder blades.

"I love you," I say, before caution and resentment can silence me.

She's smiling, although her face is still marked by tears, and her fine hair is blowing silver in the wind. "OK, then stop giving me a hard time."

"About Nora... I didn't mean..."

"Nora is no good for you. She's a flighty young thing. A cold-hearted bitch of a bird. I'm more intelligent and more talented. And richer. You'll find another seagull, plenty of other seagulls. Please don't kill yourself."

"I had no intention of killing myself."

"That's good." She kissed my lips, a touch light as feathers. "You know, Sal, it's our anniversary. I fell in love with you not far from this bridge, exactly two years ago. We went walking together in Nightingale Woods and I climbed the observatory tower. I could see you through the camera obscura, but you couldn't see me. You were sitting on the grass with this serious look on your face, watching some seagulls flying around. I knew then that I would wait for years, or however long it took..."

Her arms encircled me and I felt like a bird, gently captured and held.

Seven Swans

Seven Swans

My seven brothers turned into swans. Making a raft of their wings, they carried me from King's Cross to the South Bank. Outside the National Theatre I sat down and without wasting any time crying, began to weave coats for my brothers. Out of litter, plastic carrier bags, theatre programmes, whatever blew past. I became an accustomed oddity. Women from pity brought me their jumble-sale cast-offs, end pieces and balls of knitting wool. Men handed me empty beer cans and cigarette packets. I never rejected any possible material. Who was I to judge? I wove it all in. Now the coats are nearly finished, all except one. They've given me a certificate, for creative recycling of garbage. They want to exhibit my coats in the Tate. I smile and say nothing, in accordance with the rules. I can't speak until my work is done.

I never intended to marry. At 30, I was still happily single, working as a buyer for a major fashion chain, living in Kentish Town, in a one-bedroom flat. Then my seven brothers were discharged from (thrown out of) Caterham mental hospital, under the new Community Care regulations. Our parents being dead, I assumed the crushing responsibility for their welfare and maintenance.

Although of course they were – are – very good boys. They stayed wherever I left them each morning, not moving an inch until I returned. A discipline learnt in mental hospital. They ate pitifully little. Still, they were seven grown men, and registered as such on my Community Charge form.

So I married a stupid rich man. Without pausing to consider the practicalities, eg marital duties (sex), thinking only of my overdraft and second mortgage, I flung myself at a millionaire estate agent. He was attracted by my vivacious charm (false/assumed) and my beauty (natural).

He gave me a diamond engagement ring, it flashed with a thousand fires. Too big for any of my fingers, it reposed on a blue velvet cushion, in a hard blue box printed with silver lettering: Thompsons of Bond Street. Only later I found out the diamonds were second-hand, a legacy from his first wife, long dead. Another fairytale heroine. She cried jewels for tears. Years later, I was still finding them, behind the sofa cushions or rooted deep in the luxurious carpets. They made horrible crunchings when I hoovered.

Meanwhile I was keeping my brothers secret. When the priest asked, have you anything to declare, any just impediment, I maintained a vague smile. And they behaved immaculately. I was so proud of them. Ushers at the wedding ceremony, waiters at the reception. On our honeymoon, they travelled behind us in a small chartered plane.

All seven were now installed in a houseboat, moored at Twickenham. They liked fishing and watching the barges go up and down the river. It was only temporary, until I could find some way of explaining them to my husband.

The youngest was Joachim. I loved him best, because of his fine sensitivity and poetic soul. He limped, due to an accident at birth.

He sent me poems, with stamps drawn on the envelopes. Sometimes he just sent blank sheets of paper. They were kindly meant. I had an arrangement with the local postman.

The moon is golden blue
And the stars swim softly, like a swarm of gnats
The moon's reflection is like the river dreaming
I am like a camel without a desert

Reading this and other Small Poems by Joachim, I was plunged into grief and remorse. "What have I done?" I whispered to the driving mirror of my Mercedes. A polite electronic voice replied, in a North American accent:

The rear door is open
Please fasten your seatbelt
You are running low on gas
The rear door is open
You should never have got married
In my personal opinion
He's not right for you
Anyway, leaving this aside
Matters have not improved
Except financially
And look what money does to people
Consider your stepdaughter, for instance
If this car were a human being
And capable of emotion
It would weep for you

A seagull sweeping past overhead screeched, "Save yourself and save the poor children! Ha ha ha ha ha ha."

My stepdaughter, Clarissa, had the gift of making herself invisible, so it was easy to forget about her. But like a trapdoor spider, she would pounce out of nowhere. Although I never observed her eating she haunted Tesco, shoplifting tiny tins. Sardines and John West salmon. Warned by the seagull, a commonsensical bird despite his crazy laugh, I tried never to look at her directly, only through a small hand mirror carried for this purpose. One day in a panic I dropped the mirror and it smashed. She confronted me, smiling nastily. "Who do you love?" she demanded.

"Joachim," I said.

"Ha ha ha ha ha," cried the seagull.

Clarissa chopped the mooring rope with an axe. The houseboat went adrift, turning in slow circles, let loose at the mercy of the treacherous Thames. Seven pale faces behind the cabin windows. A small blue flag was hoisted, saying SOS. My faithful seagull was circling above. The houseboat drifted as far as Richmond Bridge, where it stuck. By the time the river police arrived to investigate, my brothers had disappeared.

"Look small," the beggarwoman advised me, as I rushed over Richmond Bridge, throwing a diamond into her outstretched hand. "Only the poor know where the poor go. Catch!" She threw me back a blue stone. Fixing it in my eye, I saw through the façade of the Richmond Riverside Development. Richmond town was like a puffed-up meringue. I ran down the artificial cobbled sidestreets. Next thing I was on a dusty platform at Piccadilly underground station, where the grey mice scurry under the electric rails. Mindful of the beggarwoman's words, I greeted them respectfully.

"Have you seen my brothers, little mice?"

"Yes, they passed through this station, earlier today. They asked us for help. We don't get much amusement down here usually. On the silly circle they go round and round. Try King's Cross."

A needle in a haystack/seven brothers on the London Underground.

I was also hunted. Clarissa was following me, and as the spider pursues the fly down intricate sticky paths, she had the Underground system at her fingertips. The indicator board at King's Cross flashed in yellow dots CIRCLE LINE 2 MINUTES. Then it flashed "She's coming. If you value your life, abandon your loved ones." O Joachim!

Clarissa appeared on the platform. People drew aside nervously, giving her a clear path towards me. She was dressed in silver, with a necklace of sharp instruments. Like a chessboard Queen.

CIRCLE LINE 1 MINUTE

Thinking fast and with the magic of desperation, I turned myself into litter and scattered myself around.

TRAIN APPROACHING

"Little mice, little mice, how can I save my brothers now, from the evil witch, my wicked stepdaughter?"

"Squeak squeak, we can't help you any more. Don't be a litter bug. Remember the terrible King's Cross fire."

Unluckily, Clarissa overheard our whispered conference. Her eyes gleamed menacingly. Think fast!

I turned myself into a chocolate-dispensing machine. She rattled my drawers and poked sharp things into me. I became a poster warning about drugs. She wrote graffiti on me. O Joachim!

The train doors stuck, giving me a moment's grace. I turned

back into my human self and grabbed Clarissa by the throat, intending to strangle her. Then a tiny voice in my submerged or higher consciousness, or it might have been the seagull, cried: "You are not natural enemies. Clarissa is your true sister. Remember the feminist movement of the late 1960s and 1970s. Whatever happened to love between women?"

Yes, what did happen to it?

I took a risk and instead of strangling Clarissa, I kissed her on the lips. Instantly she turned into Sinéad O'Connor, don't ask me why.

The train doors opened, out fell my brothers. Our joyful reunion was interrupted by the ticket inspectors. So I turned my brothers into swans and they flew with me above the peaked caps of the inspectors, up the down escalator and over the automatic barriers into the dark blue night sky pierced with stars bright as diamonds.

I finished the coats on New Year's Eve, all except for one sleeve. As Big Ben chimed midnight, I threw them over my seven swan brothers, who reassumed their true original forms. Joachim was offered a job by an international tour company, showing American sightseers around London. They love the wing.

Cheese

Cheese

If I'd been a totally flesh-and-blood girl, if I'd not compromised my own material, would she have stayed with me? Or found some other reason for leaving?

I wonder if I should feel sad. The cheese part of me – three-quarters now – doesn't mourn her, doesn't care. The other 25% is uncertain.

The truth is, she didn't like me not to be natural, but that word meant different things to us. Early in our relationship, for instance, I acquired blonde highlights. A vegetable dye, the hairdresser reassured me. It was mainly spruce, derived from the bark of that common evergreen. I liked the idea of being partly a tree. Standing with the other spruces on some northern hillside, quiet and close together. Making a silent, dark conifer space where humans would be afraid to walk, their chatter stilled, and carpeting the peaty soil with our discarded needles.

Sylvia was horrified. Bouffant hair and blonde highlights – I wasn't her kind of girlfriend. "A tree died, just so you could look like Marilyn Monroe!"

Oh. I hadn't thought of it that way. I'd assumed the bark was "harvested", as they strip cork trees in Portugal every nine years. Or that my tree would perhaps have been felled for some other reason, to make rafters or tables, the dye merely a by-product. But she linked the earth's despoliation and women's – my – vanity. Those blonde highlights did most unfortunately change her view of me. From natural to artificial. From gentle and fairly harmless to a rampant destructive force.

Even now I'm wondering, could our relationship have been saved by intervention of some kind? Sylvia would never have agreed to counselling. She scorned the use of techniques to resuscitate feelings, to jump-start emotional batteries.

Meanwhile, *fromage* transplants were becoming ever more sophisticated. I don't know why they called the surgical process *fromage*; the French word served no euphemistic purpose since everyone knew what it meant. The French called it cheese, *le cheese-technique*. It came from America, like everything. It caught on first among supermodels, pop stars and the wives of rich businessmen. Cheese could be smoothed to make a flat stomach, or moulded into breasts of whatever shape and colour. Cheese sex would leave you feeling full and satisfied. If you liked cheese – but everyone did then, or pretended to.

Cheese into flesh, flesh into cheese. This marvellous new material, though produced by cows, had been transformed by scientists, all its less desirable aspects neutralised. Everybody wanted it now, except Sylvia. Rubbery, blue-veined or marbled. Fashion is a crazy thing (but a human thing?) – that desire to be like others, to remake oneself in their image, to conform.

Treatment was soon freely available and much cheaper. My breasts cost only six months' wages after tax. At the same time the surgeon replaced the glands under my arms. Two of my aunts died of breast cancer. If it was that or go dairy, which would you choose?

It was weeks before Sylvia found out. She was sleeping in the spare bedroom. Instincts of mistrust. I seemed false to her – false, the worst thing she thought anybody could be. She valued honesty above all. I never know what people mean by that word.

I expected shock, outrage, disgust. But she was just really upset. She took off her glasses, those funny old-fashioned plastic-framed specs she insists on wearing – says they feel comfortable – and rubbed her eyes, in a defeated way. "What will you get next?" she asked. "A heart of cheese?"

I laughed.

"Cheese brains? Or d'you have those already?" She opened the fridge door and glanced inside.

"It won't affect things... it shouldn't..."

"Things?"

"You and me. I mean..."

"How about you and reality? Or was that just a brief encounter?"

I felt a twinge of nostalgia, as though she'd mentioned an old schoolfriend. Reality – a girl with a missing front tooth and a way of peering at you from behind her fringe. A bit taciturn, but whatever she did say would be worth listening to.

"And what about the baby?" Sylvia asked.

"The baby?"

"You're pregnant, remember?"

So I was – five months.

"How are you going to feed her? Bottle?"

"No, look..." I ran to fetch the instruction booklet they'd given me after the operation. It had these amazing diagrams. But I returned to an empty kitchen.

I watched a lot of cheese porn in my third trimester. I was feeling lonely. Even the video shop owner had started giving me disapproving looks. But since I'd never been perfect before, why should the pregnant me assume an air of false virtue? I was no one's Virgin Mary – at least, my child would have the DNA of two (in fact three) parents. I would always feel grateful to Sylvia for this, for giving me Selina.

In the meantime I just felt depressed. Empty inside, though stuffed to the gills with baby. Cheese porn crammed my mind in turn with garish bright images. I watched many people being eaten – their sexual and other organs, their fingers and toes, their lips and noses. Their breasts.

My own breasts hadn't cottoned on yet. They weren't changing shape, or leaking. Despite all the scientific hype, they didn't *know*. Stupid cheese, I found myself thinking.

I missed Sylvia, who'd gone to stay in a chalet by a lake. Rediscovering her soul in the wilderness. To reach that wilderness she'd taken a taxi, the tube to Heathrow airport, a plane, another plane, another taxi. She'd changed currency and bought travellers' cheques, plus all the equipment necessary to lead the simple life, to absorb the infinite.

Meanwhile the finite absorbed me and prepared to exit from my body. She too was impatient to escape. Women, I thought, squeezing out a tear of self-pity. Always leaving, on their way to somewhere else. Women and tears. I didn't feel like a woman to myself, though my breasts now exuded a thin whey. Some new monstrous creature, that's what I'd become. And yet this was natural.

Slug Heaven

Slug Heaven

... and to everything that creepeth upon the earth, wherein there is life, I have given every green herb for meat. Genesis 2:30

I'd heard many things about Slug Heaven, before ever I got the chance to go there myself. I'd been told that in that garden grew every kind of fruit and variety of vegetable. No traps are set, no poisons laid down, so I was told. On the contrary – in that garden, slugs are welcomed as guests. The table is laid for us, the cupboard is full, the host is gracious.

Furthermore, they said, the soil is pure London clay. Here you may slumber undisturbed, safe in your cool chamber – no busy worm comes here, no prodding ant. A miraculous dew falls every night, freshening and lubricating the grass. Moist, all is moist and slimy, gluey and mucilaginous!

I dreamed then, a dream of unimpeded delight. As I was sliding along, the grass parted to show a purple flower, the immortal amaranth. Then the voice of God spoke. "Thou art my beloved slug, in whom I am well pleased. Through thee, oh slug, sinful Nature is redeemed. Take just one bite of this blessed flower – then chew, swallow and fully ingest."

I reared up towards the flower. Stretching, yearning. "Open wide!" the voice instructed, with a kindly chuckle. Yes I, a simple slug, heard God's laughter...

I used to live in Slug Hell – a fiercely tended, savagely raked, pesticide-sprayed kind of place, where any weed so foolhardy as to extend a runner or crack a seed would be torn up shrieking like a blackbird. Or not – for weeds are generally quiet sorts of chaps, not given to hysterics like your overbred garden varieties. Quiet as martyrs. Silently resigned to their fate as Early Christians. But that's another story, from one of my former lives. Not relevant. Mustn't get distracted.

The thing is, a green and tangled covert of weeds is like a five-star hotel to us slugs. With air-conditioning. Curled up happily snoozing, safe from the midday sun's excruciations, all kinds of mouth-oozing food growing close by. Not the weeds, I don't mean them, of course! A slug wouldn't eat a weed unless he was desperate. Why not? – you ask. Why not be the gardener's little biological friend, smiles all round? Well, a weed by its nature is accidental and tastes raw, uncultivated. We prefer things grown on purpose.

Two personal tragedies in succession resolved me to attempt an escape from 66 Gehenna Close (cul-de-sac), off Acheron Way, Styx-in-the-Wold. First, my revered mother – Mumsy, of legendary size and fertility – fell prey to the wiles of the Foul Fiend, Mr Smyth-Jones. In an absent-minded moment while grazing she first licked, then crunched, one of those radioactive rocks, those little blue time bombs he scatters along our ancient routes. She enjoyed her breakfast, before dying in agony.

I don't suppose anybody reading this will understand or care (or will they? Will this little personal memoir, this plea on behalf of a small and oppressed though multiplying species, perhaps touch some human heart?) just how hard it was. Finding Mumsy dead, I mean that was bad enough. But then, for fear of poisoning, not being able to do the natural, desirable, filial thing. I couldn't even risk a nibble. So her corpse remained where it lay, unconsumed – oh blasphemy and eternal shame! – until removed with fastidious tongs by Mr Smyth-Jones.

Next, the plastic bag incident. I won't go into details. No doubt my human readers can find some defence or excuse for Mr S-J's cruelty. But how would you feel if someone put between fifteen and twenty of your relatives in a plastic bag and then poured boiling water in the bag, turning your nearest and dearest to gloop?

Yet even in the midst of carnage and genocide I refused to let my spirit be squashed. There was, I knew, a better place out there somewhere. Slug Heaven! I became preoccupied – you might say obsessed – with the idea of finding this promised land, this new Eden. And while lost in fantasies of poppies eager in my mouth, of forward young hostas and delphiniums who wouldn't take no for an answer, stupidly I neglected to keep an eye out for predators. A thrush hopped down the path and speared me through the pneumostome. So I died and I, or rather my spirit, went to Slug Heaven. No, I'm lying. I made a bargain with the thrush, following which he carried me half a mile, then dropped me into the garden for whose delights I'd hungered. In return I did something I'm not proud of. To be revealed.

"All wars are about land," said the She. "The world is overpopulated. People should stop breeding." She patted her huge belly. The He smirked.

"No, seriously, Greg. What right have we to claim this as our land, our garden? They were here first."

"We pay the mortgage. I haven't noticed any slugs offering to contribute."

"Oh, look!" she cried, spotting me as I glided cautiously out from behind a rustic trough. "There's one now – a golden one. It's come to say hello!"

I contracted in alarm and went all rubbery. "I think I'll call him Sebastian. We won't hurt you, don't worry, little Sebastian."

"Sebastian Slug!" he snorted. I heard him go back inside the house.

I liked the name. It had a formal dignity. Cautiously, I extended my optical tentacles and popped my eyes out the top. She was still watching me. I twiddled my sensory tentacles in a flirtatious manner. After all, this was Slug Heaven. Different rules applied. It didn't seem impossible that a fertile female of the human species should fall for a handsome young slug – one such as I. Golden, she'd called me. A prince among slugs.

"Sebastian, dear," she cooed in wood pigeon-like tones. "I know you love tomatoes. But we'd like a few as well, to put in our salads. So please can I ask you a big, big favour? Will you and your little friends leave just one tomato plant alone – that tall one in the middle of the row?"

But that's the best one! – I couldn't stop myself ignobly thinking.

"I know that plant has loads more tomatoes than the others, so it's a bit unfair, but you and the other little sluggy-wuggies can eat all the rest," she replied to my thoughts, as if we were somehow linked, woman and slug, by some invisible force like psychic slime. Creepy! Thrilling!

"Thanks for your help, Sebastian. I really appreciate it." She levered herself upright, balancing her enormous egg sac, and lumbered indoors.

Oh, great. Now I'd really landed myself in the deepest manure. Why would the other slugs pay any attention to me – a newcomer, still dry under the mantle? Besides, they were disaffected enough already. I'd never met such a load of moaning molluscs. "Call this Paradise?" they'd grumble. "Where's the ambrosia, then? Where's the honey-dew?" Frequent reference was made also to the "She-Before", an elderly female regarded among them as some kind of earth goddess. Oh, the cornucopia she'd provided! The salads, the rows of seedlings, the exotic fruits and other rare delicacies. Oh generosity unstinted, benevolence overflowing – she'd practically fed them by hand. Swollen, surfeited, they'd rolled from appetiser to main course to dessert, then on through *les autres plats du jour*. Well, after that you can understand that a few tomatoes (when in season), two spindly rows of lettuces and the occasional bucket of vegetable peelings dumped in the compost bin held little appeal.

"What happened to her, the She-Before?" I idly asked one of my new associates. "Did she die?"

"Yeah, murdered by MI5," he apathetically revealed. "Knew too many state secrets."

Having curled myself around the base of the middle tomato plant, I found it fairly easy to keep the others at bay, by threatening violence. "Easy, old chap!" they attempted to soothe me. "Steady on, mate!" And then: "Oh, please yourself."

I resolved not to leave my post until the She had picked and enjoyed all her rightful tomatoes. But alas! My Nemesis appeared in the garden at daybreak – the thrush with which I'd sealed a previous fateful bargain. May as well give you the details. For that dread bird I'd called up worms – yes, innocent worms, lured unsuspecting by my song of enchantment, the very tune and lyrics warbled by my slug ancestors upon the dawning of the First Day. They poked their blind heads curiously above ground, then emerged and swayed together in a merry dance. Thrush spaghetti.

I consented now to sing again, under threat of being flown back to Slug Hell. (Alas! Would that I'd chosen that less evil fate).

Directly after the second Massacre of Worms, while still cowering under a leaf I heard the She go past. "Oh no!" she cried. Of course her tomato plants were simply covered in slugs, the middle one too. They'd stormed the citadel while my attention was distracted.

Deep-mantled shame – for having deserted my post, muffed my allotted task – was soon replaced by alarm. She groaned, said "Ow!" and clutched her egg sac. "Are you all right?" called the He.

"It's starting!"

He helped her inside. I was left alone to brood upon the possible consequences of my sin. Would my beloved die and would it be my fault – would her murder fall upon my soul, already stained crimson with the blood of thirty or so worms? When proactive in the first massacre, at least I could comfort myself that the disgrace belonged to my old Slug Hellish life. Though truly a crime against Nature, it was committed in an unnatural, denaturalised environment. That was perhaps some excuse. But now, to have desecrated Slug Heaven itself by my actions!

Despair numbed me for a day and a night – then I was seized by a savage hunger. Never since my second incarnation as a lion have I felt such urgent appetite. To sink my teeth – ah, teeth! – into the sweet, tender flesh of an Early Christian martyr. And believe me, those Early Christians weren't thrown to us poor starving beasts any too often, in Nero's amphitheatre.

I rampaged through the vegetable patch. If I was bad, so be it! I could still have fun. I climbed the main stem of the middle tomato plant, settled in the fork of a branch and started eating.

Not long after, I heard the chatter of human females. The She and another. The She was reclining on the sofa, holding to her breast something which at first glance I took for a huge slug. Yes, similarities between us and human beings may be noted at times. The He's Thing – which is often on view, owing to his habit of standing naked in the open French windows – also looks remarkably slug-like. The windows stood ajar now, so I could hear every word.

"Your garden's getting terribly overgrown. I'll tackle it while I'm here. Lucky I brought my secateurs."

"Oh, but Mum, that's how I like it. I want a sort of wild garden…"

"It looks messy. And you'll encourage slugs, with all those weeds."

"I don't mind the slugs, they've got as much right to be here as we have…"

"Nonsense! Do be practical. To hear you talk, anybody would think it was wrong to kill slugs. Oh what a silly mummy you've got, coochy-coo. No, darling, you have to be ruthless in this world. You can either have slugs and snails or you can have a garden, it's a simple choice. I'd usually scatter slug pellets, but we don't want to run the risk of baby eating anything nasty by mistake, do we? So if I see any, I'll just chop them in half. Quick and easy. And organic! They don't feel any pain. Look at that huge one right now on your best tomato plant."

Myself compromised and guilty, I could hardly blame my beloved for colluding in genocide (every species for itself) – nor hope, as that vile, grinning woman advanced across the garden towards me, slipping back the safety catch on her secateurs, that after death I might find myself in a better place.

Neighbours

Neighbours

The day I discovered that Olive next door had stolen my trampoline – and had been bouncing on it! – was the same day that Margery from up the road invited me to a Christian meeting.

This neighbourhood is not very neighbourly, or else I'm not. When I saw an elderly woman with a familiar face coming towards me along a narrow bit of pavement between the fence and the unruly Nature Strip, I waved awkwardly and dodged out of the way behind a big holly bush. She had never seemed particularly friendly and we'd never talked. To my surprise, however, she skipped around the other side of the bush and we met in the road.

"Hello, I'm Margery. I've seen you going up and down – tell me, do you live round here? Did I meet you at Ruth's get-together?" she enquired.

"Er, no. I live at number 81."

"And have you been here very long?"

"Not very. Six years," I said apologetically, knowing six years to be a mere nothing in the eyes of Stainmore Park Drive. Three or four decades seems to be the average. "What about you?"

"Oh, I'm not one of the *real* old guard," Margery said. "I moved

115

here in 1964. When we were first married, my husband and I lived in Hackney. I brought up my children in two rooms in Stoke Newington. I had to save hard to get a bigger place..."

This sounded interesting and I hoped she would continue telling me her life story, but she then changed tack. "I don't want to load Christianity on you, but let me tell you about these meetings we have at the local church..."

All at once my mind cleared of confusion, as I perceived her motive for buttonholing me. Not betraying disappointment – hardly even feeling it – I focused on keeping an alert expression pinned to my face.

"It's mainly for young people trying to find their way in the world..."

I wondered if she thought *I* was young. Margery's face is deeply wrinkled, the once soft cushions of her cheeks and chin collapsed to fleshy bags. I could feel the skin stretching back from my own eyes and the lines scored across my forehead and etched either side of my mouth. Though I might be a quarter century behind Margery, I'm not young.

Meanwhile she was telling me about the home-cooked food provided at these Alpha meetings and how the atmosphere was friendly and non-pressurising. An opportunity for getting to know our neighbours. She would put a leaflet through my door, she said, and so we parted. I went home to find a message on my answerphone from one of my brothers, expressing interest in how I was getting on and asking if by any chance I could babysit that evening, as their arrangements had fallen through at the last moment.

Is this what modern life consists of, I wondered bitterly. The sting in the tail of the apparent friendliness – that people always want something, are not really interested in you at all. Or is it human nature? I rang my brother and sister-in-law back and left an effusive but regretful message on their answerphone.

Then I sat on the sofa and stared at the dusty artificial coal fireplace, thinking how life was full of petty irritations. For instance, why hadn't my trampoline arrived yet? Maybe I should ring the crazy sales agent. She was also evangelical, only about trampolines. Within five minutes of our first telephone conversation – I got her number from a newspaper article – she had talked me up a model. She even tried to persuade me to buy two, one for home use and the other for work! She quoted statistics at me: 80% of people hardly ever use their exercise bikes, etc. A trampoline in contrast, she pointed out, requires no complicated assembly, is always ready to be bounced on, can double as a coffee table.

I began to worry about my phone bill, as when last year I spent so long on the phone to Enfield Council that BT suggested nominating them as my Best Friend.

Three days later she rang me. Had my trampoline arrived yet? No, it hadn't.

"We've just had the results of our customer satisfaction survey, which you might be interested to know about..."

I looked at my watch. It was after 10pm. "I'm sorry but I'm just on my way to bed."

"Oh. All right then," she said, in a slightly hostile way.

That was five days ago and the trampoline had still not turned up, so I took a deep breath and rang her. "Oh yes," she said, still with a trace of resentment. "You're the lady who wanted an early night. Well, I'll check with our delivery firm."

She rang back. "They have delivered it. Your neighbour at 79 took it in."

Just then, I heard again a peculiar noise, which I had previously been unable to account for, coming through the party wall. A rhythmic squeaking. It was coming from Olive's sitting room.

At once I realised the truth, but my mind rejected it as being incredible. Certainly beyond the bounds of acceptable behaviour.

My trampoline! Being used by Olive!

Energetically, it sounded like.

I charged out around the front, pressed my neighbour's bell hard and rattled her letterbox.

After a long pause she opened the door. Her face was flushed and she was wearing – or had just pulled around her for modesty's sake – a pink quilted dressing-gown.

"Have you got my trampoline?"

"What trampoline?" she asked, looking guilty.

"The one they tried to deliver the other day. Addressed to me. That you took in."

"Oh, that one!"

It's hard to feel angry with somebody in her sixties and quite plump, who when in her curlers – as she was – resembles Mrs Tiggywinkle.

"You've had it all the time! Why didn't you let me know, so I could come and collect it?"

"Oh, I thought they'd put a note through your door," Olive explained, lying blatantly. "I waited, but you never came round. So I thought you didn't want it. Well, you can have it now."

I followed her down the hallway, into her neat sitting-room, crammed with china ornaments and photographs of grandchildren. There it was, standing on the pale green carpet, between the television and the French windows. Its springs must have only just stopped vibrating.

We both inspected it, standing side by side. "A bit shop-soiled..." Olive mused.

"Yes, because you've been bouncing on it."

"What me? At my age? Linda, can you seriously accuse me?"

"Well, someone has," I said sternly. "Who do you suggest, if not you?"

Olive's eyes slid towards the cat – a rotund tabby, snoozing on the sofa. This animal, Flossie, gets prawns every day and a saucer-ful of cream.

I made an impatient noise and Olive gave up trying to deceive me. "Do you want the packing it came in?" she asked, in a small defeated voice.

"Yes, please."

"It's upstairs, waiting to go in the attic. My son-in-law kindly volunteered... my arthritis has been troubling me and I thought it might help," she said, plaintively reverting to the trampoline. "I only had one little go on it. Was that such a terrible crime?"

Climbing the stairs, she heaved a sigh. "I'll think carefully next time, before putting myself out to help one of my neighbours..."

So in the end my trampoline reached its proper destination, according to all legal rules and principles of natural justice – my sitting-room, not Olive's. But my righteous indignation soon ebbed away, leaving me feeling a bit lost.

I thought I would go to the Alpha meeting, after all. No harm in taking a look; peering out from behind the net curtains of my mistrustful, settled life.

Of course I ran the risk of being possessed by the spirit of Christian lunacy, but this was unlikely to happen. I had striven for so long, over so many dreary years, to achieve the appearance of being sane and normal. And had succeeded. Bearing my powerful shield of appearance, I could go anywhere now and be invulnerable.

No, my heart would not be filled with the Lord. I was too middle-aged for that game. And too bogged down by material concerns.

A woman of pure and generous heart would simply have shelled out for another trampoline, I thought – thus pleasing both Olive and the sales agent. A Christian woman with a large bank balance.

I gazed sadly at the trampoline. Remembering the energetic squeaking sound – a happy sound – I'd heard through the wall. Thinking how Olive was to be admired, in a way. She lived her life to the full, with zest. I couldn't work up that amount of enthusiasm for anything, certainly not trampolining. In fact, I'd completely gone off the whole idea. Was I still within the 15-day approval period, I wondered? Would I be eligible for a refund?

The letterbox clicked. My Alpha leaflet lay on the doormat.

An opportunity to explore the meaning of life, it said. The Alpha Course – starting soon at a church near you.

Alpha is a short, practical, no frills, introduction to the Christian faith.

What is the point of life? What happens when we die? Is forgiveness possible? What relevance does Jesus have for our lives today?

For some reason my eyes had filled with tears, so the words swam together and I read Olive by mistake for our lives.

What relevance does Jesus have for Olive today?

Good question.

What fragile threads stretch between us? Would Olive be interested in accompanying me to an evening of learning and laughter, including a delicious meal of home-cooked food? The leaflet said we might be asked for a contribution to the meal. I would pay Olive's contribution, if we could let bygones be bygones and she felt like coming along.

Red Office

Red Office

One week, over several consecutive days, our office was painted red. No, it was mainly painted a peculiar colour called Serenade, like vomit, someone said, except that vomit can be different colours, so this was not a precise description. Like oyster or magnolia, the colour of a cheaply converted flat, all smooth and shining, before ominous patches of damp appear where the rain is overflowing from the blocked-up gutters and penetrating the walls. Yes, exactly that colour, but enlivened in our office's case by dashes of bright and lurid red – red pillars, red filing cabinets and red radiators.

Word got around. People made special visits from the first, third and fourth floors to view the dramatic spectacle. They blinked and smiled uncertainly, or laughed loudly. Carol said that our filing cabinets were the talk of the lately established smoking room in the basement, its walls sticky with nicotine, air heavy with gossip and fumes, where Grace might be found, if through hurt pride I were not avoiding her, because she cancelled our lunch date and talks to other people in union meetings.

The new colour scheme was Luke's idea, because the colour red motivates people, or so he told Muriel, his secretary. Luke does not enjoy a calm office atmosphere, no, he stirs the murky depths of the settled pond, he pokes the ants' nest, or it might be said he revels in the use and misuse of power.

After suffering a severe headache two days running, I traced its source to the red pillar situated directly behind my Apple Mac. "A number of factors may contribute to cause eye strain, including seemingly insignificant matters such as the office colour scheme" I read in a Health & Safety Executive booklet on new technology. It seemed reasonable to suppose that if red motivated people, it might also give them headaches. I went to get some paracetamol from the first-aid cupboard, but it was locked and Philip Sidney of the computer department informed me that anyway it was empty of useful drugs, in accordance with EC regulations, to guard against the possibility of staff, whether by accident or by design, taking fatal overdoses and their grieving relatives bringing legal actions against the company.

The first-aid cupboard now contained only a couple of bandages, judged harmless, and a tiny blue-glass bottle of smelling salts, as used by bridesmaids at royal weddings. The first-aid book dangled on a piece of dirty string above the photocopier, permanently open to announce that "On 2 July 1987, at 10.30am in the PRD administration offices, 1st floor, a ceiling tile fell off and hit Iris Hancock on the head whilst she was sending a fax. Although shocked, she was not badly injured and will not require hospital treatment". No further entries, although surely some minor injuries had been sustained in the five years since Iris was assaulted by a piece of polystyrene. The glue on those tiles is no more reliable now than it was in the late 1980s, although to the sharp-eyed observer they give clear warning signs of their impending detachment. Threatened with redundancy in these post-Depression years, dragging ourselves into work with period pains, cured of Monday and Friday-itis, staying grimly till 6 or 7pm, maybe we also find it harder to admit to physical injury. "20 May 1986. Jane Marsden was fetching an elastoplast for a colleague with a cut finger; the lid of the first-aid cabinet failed to open properly at first, then fell down sharply, cutting her head. There was a small amount of blood."

I stuck pieces of A4 white paper to my red pillar with sellotape, effectively screening the section of it that was giving me a headache. Feeling pleased with this solution, I then wrote on it "Headache pillar" in green felt-tip pen. It was now beginning to re-semble a surrealist work of art. My colleagues looked at it, then at me, in fearful apprehension – they already knew I was odd, but now it occurred to them, I might have a serious mental illness. "Has Luke seen that?" Carol asked. She is my immediate boss, one down from Luke in the office hierarchy, so it was her responsibil-ity, we both knew, to tell me to remove the paper, but she was pissed off with Luke because he keeps cancelling important meet-ings at short notice; this counted in my favour.

"He hasn't been in today," I replied, disingenuously. Luke op-erates an efficient spy network: his personal eyes might not have rested on my pillar, but its transformation would certainly have been described to him, in hurried phone calls.

"Well, it all seems very petty," Carol said. "Couldn't you just ignore the pillar?"

"No, I'm sorry, but you see it stands right behind my computer, in my direct line of sight, so I'm sorry, but I can't possibly ignore it."

Carol repressed a smile. "You know, the decorators painted a pil-lar red in Luke's room by mistake and he was so furious, he ordered them to repaint it straight away. I heard him shouting at them at six o'clock yesterday morning – telling them it was contrary to his clear instructions and an insult."

Insult. The word reminded me of hospitals, my father and the medical phrase "an insult to the brain". Wiping out the body's memory, like the Etch-a-Sketch, that expensive toy he once allowed me to have, the plastic screen with two knobs you could turn to make angular scribbles, then shake the screen to see its miraculous powers of erasure.

"Well, it is an insult," I said "to think you can motivate your employees with red paint, instead of pay rises." Our managing director had circulated a memo to all staff, expressing his smooth regret that there would be no pay reviews this year, due to recent "extraordinary expenditure" – in particular, the cost of redecorating the building. Adding injury to insult. "Why were you in here at six o'clock in the morning?" I asked.

"Oh, you know, Luke gets in early and it makes a good impression. As I mentioned to you in your quarterly assessment, Annie, we not only have to do our jobs, we have to be seen to be doing them. Make that a conscious and deliberate part of your career strategy. And by the way..."

Muriel came in, waving a knife. Its blade flashed under the fluorescent lights. "I can't stand it any more," she said, her breath coming fast and shallow, her forehead shiny below her parted and strained-back hair. "They're all picking on me and talking about me behind my back, the atmosphere's terrible, it's like a witch hunt."

Carol slipped into her office and closed the door. With her career in mind, she would not wish to be seen associating with Muriel, a stroppy, independent-minded woman and therefore an obvious target for victimisation by Luke's sycophants. The writing was on the wall, or on the red pillar – Luke would sack her soon. In fact, as I happened to have noticed while scanning the job columns of the local free newspaper, he had already placed an advertisement for a new secretary. Muriel was going on holiday next week, so the preliminary interviews were probably scheduled for then.

"So I've brought the post in here to open." Muriel sat down at an adjacent desk and began slitting a pile of envelopes. "My faith gives me strength, otherwise I'd probably top myself. But I'm a Christian."

Muriel often tells me she is a Christian, in a low, prideful voice, as if revealing a special secret close to her heart. Once I almost reciprocated by confiding that I was a lesbian, but as I think she belongs to some evangelical sect, I am glad I kept my mouth shut.

"Maybe I'll start applying for other jobs."

"That's a good idea."

"Because I might be paranoid, but I think he's looking for an excuse to sack me. For instance, the night before last, I worked till past eight o'clock doing the media packs like he'd told me to, and at half-past seven, the phone rang. Well, I knew it must be him, checking up on me – who else would ring the office at half-past seven? I was going to answer it, but then I decided, no, I'm too busy to play stupid games. I don't need to justify myself. So I just let it ring. And the next day, before I'd even had a chance to say good morning, he called me all sorts of vile names, accusing me of having left early. But I told him, 'I was here, I must have been down at the photocopier when you rang'. And he can't prove I wasn't, can he?"

"Why should you stay till half-past seven, anyway? You don't get paid overtime. The bastard."

"I think he's planning something."

By now it was lunchtime, so I went for a walk in the park. I was suffering from a painful fit of unrequited love, the kind I commonly get in late autumn, but this particular attack had lasted three years already, its intensity not noticeably diminishing with the changing of the seasons. Grace must know how I felt about her, otherwise why had she cancelled our arrangement to go for a lunchtime drink? Besides, I blush easily and my face is as WYSIWYG as my Apple Mac screen. No, the only thing to do was to avoid her scrupulously from this day forward, to preserve my last remnants of dignity by never again using the PRD photocopier even if ours was genuinely out of order and going straight down the back stairs to the sandwich queue, rather than taking the slightly longer route along the first corridor, in the hope of catching a glimpse of her.

I crossed a stream and began sloshing uphill towards the wood. The park is the country kind as opposed to the urban. It incorporates a golf course and a miniature farm, as well as most of Middlesex University. Students were out combing the grass for magic mushrooms; they held small plastic bags and looked seriously intent. In the wind, rain and fresh air, my head began to clear, my heart to lift. The park is a reliably work-free zone, since my colleagues toil through their lunch hours or go to the pub. Once Muriel asked me dubiously if I wasn't frightened of being attacked. No, I feel safer out here.

Muriel, Luke, Carol, Philip Sidney and even Grace were all, it occurred to me, if not exactly figments of my imagination, yet aspects of my karma, of the imprisoning morass of earthly concerns and preoccupations within which my soul struggles, like a seagull caught in an oil slick.

I had the foreboding sense of something being about to happen. Some minor or perhaps major disaster. Already that week I had witnessed a masked raid on a security van and seen a chimney fall off a block of flats. Misfortunes tend to come in threes, don't they?

Musing thus, I almost tripped over two Middlesex University students, male and female, lying entwined in the long wet grass. They were both wearing duffle coats and jeans, untoggled and unzipped. Careless passion. I'm 36, I thought, and I've never made love in a duffle coat. Life is passing/has passed me by. I wish I had a lover. Or even a friend, yes, a friend would be nice. I did have some, but they seemed far away. In another Travelcard zone or lifetime. What I needed was a friend within the company. Then I would feel less of a misfit, less lonely.

Arriving back in the office, I found a note on my desk from Carol. "Annie, I have gone home to catch up on a huge backlog of work. Please tidy up the office, *put your disks in the disk holder*, clear all the work surfaces and leave nothing on your desk when you go home tonight."

So. Carol was taking the afternoon off and I would have peace, for what remained of Friday. Even the Busy Bees playgroup had packed up for the day, leaving the neighbouring church hall sombre. Likewise the builders, who over the past several years have been mending the church's flat roof, had removed their asphalt sheeting, their tar buckets and themselves. The weathercock had seemingly flown away too, an illusion that occurs whenever it turns on its steeple point to the north-west. I thought I might practise my yoga exercises in this lovely solitude.

A piece of paper fluttered to the floor, from the desk next to mine. A leaf from a notepad, with a pretty blue flower printed in the corner. "Let the wicked be ashamed, and be brought down to hell. Let deceitful lips be made dumb. (Psalm 30, A prayer of a just man under affliction.)" I recognised the neat handwriting as Muriel's. While reading it, and wondering how close to the edge she was, I felt the first twinges of a tension headache. Something just beyond my range of vision was making strenuous efforts to be noticed. Like a silent shout, or a loud silence. I looked up. My red pillar had been stripped naked, its paper veil torn down by violent, hasty hands and crumpled in the bin. Only a scrap of sellotape remained.

I began to tremble. This is war, I told myself. Luke is trying to break my spirit, to crush me. Well, he's got a choice, it's this pillar or me. Me or the bloody colour scheme.

Muriel stood in the doorway. "I know who was responsible for that," she said. "It was..."naming one of Luke's henchmen. "I just had a phone call from His Majesty. He dictated a memo to me, saying I was sacked. I've got to type it up. He's coming in to sign it later this afternoon."

"Oh, Muriel!" I went over and tentatively put my arms around her. It was like trying to hug a rock. Her eyes blazed with a strange, distant light. "You must take it to a tribunal."

"The Lord is my tribunal."

She went out again. Muriel was stronger than me, she could endure being alone at such a time. Tears were streaming down my face. He is a madman, I thought, a serial killer, he is like Robert Maxwell, he enjoys hurting people, destroying our lives, it gives him a kick. I paced back and forth. Then I found myself downstairs in Grace's office, without exactly understanding how I'd got there. I had been aiming for the coffee machine.

Grace looked exhausted. She was writing out sticky labels for the filing cabinets, in a desultory way. PRD had recently moved two doors up the corridor. Their office, too, had that Friday afternoon deserted feeling. I sat on an upturned plastic crate. She gave me a cigarette, with instructions to waft the smoke out of the window. She has pale skin and light red hair, a beautiful, soothing shade of red, quite different from my pillar, and clear, perceiving eyes, so unlike Carol's or Luke's.

"The man's a right prick, isn't he?" she said, when I paused for breath. "Tell Muriel to get herself straight along to the Citizen's Advice Bureau."

"She's placing her faith in the Lord."

"Fuck that." Grace has an extreme antipathy to things religious; even the word "spiritual" makes her jerk backwards in disgust. "What a place this is, eh, everyone's a bloody nutter. On your corridor." She laughed, pulled a cigarette from the packet and lit it, tipping her chair back. "So how are you, anyway? Haven't seen you for ages."

By your choice, not mine, I thought, but managed to restrain myself from saying. Safer to dodge the main issue, as usual. Immediately you develop a crush on someone, it completely ruins your prospects of having an intelligent conversation with her, of getting to know her better. It reaches the point, as a friend of mine observed, where you're not even sure if you like her any more – and you're *still* behaving like a plonker.

I do like her. It's myself I have severe doubts about.

I opened my mouth, hoping a coherent sentence would emerge, although the blood was now fizzing through my veins like lemonade and my heart was the squeezed lemon, but fortunately I was interrupted by noises above. Voices rising in a crescendo, followed by a crash.

"Bloody hell!" Grace leapt to her feet. We both stared at the ceiling. In the square gap left by a long-ago-fallen polystyrene tile, a red stain was spreading. Slowly it spread wider. It filled the square. Like a Rothko painting. Like a bleed ad. Darker in the centre. A drop splashed down on Grace's desk.

"Is that red paint?" she said.

"No. Grace," I said, "I think I'm in love with you."

Grace walked round the desk and took a grip on my arm. "Annie," she said, "you're not. What you are is bored. Frustrated in your job, isolated in your office. And I'm the only other dyke within a quarter mile radius."

Something big fell past the window. A black dustbin bag. Gretchen, the cleaner, throws them out of the office windows into the skip in the car park. Starting on the fourth floor.

"What d'you think's happened?" Grace changed the subject, but kept a reassuring hold on me.

"Muriel's got a knife. She uses it for opening the post."

"Hmm. Of course, he might just be badly wounded. I guess we should go and investigate."

As we reached the second-floor landing, Grace said thoughtfully, "The laws on provocation are shockingly biased against women. Although it's getting better – a woman who beat her husband to death with a rolling pin and buried him in the garden got off with two years' probation last year. Mental state impaired by years of sustained abuse. Muriel could offer the same defence."

"But Luke's not violent, at least not physically. He's just a bully."

"Yeah, but men get off scot-free after killing their 'nagging wives'."

"That's domestic violence."

"We live here, most of the time."

All the lights were off along our corridor and the street lamps cast an eerie orange glow through the outer offices. As Grace pushed open the swing door, Muriel emerged from Luke's private office, buttoning up her coat.

"Oh, hello." She looked at us, blankly. "I was just going home."

"Muriel, um, are you all right?" I faltered.

"Fine, thanks."

"We heard a noise... like someone falling on the floor..."

"Oh, did you?" She locked Luke's office door and slipped the key into her coat pocket.

"Has Luke been in?"

"Oh yes. We parted on good terms. Agreeing to disagree. It's the Lord's will," she added, ambiguously. "He has pointed out a new path for me. I'm going to Africa, to be a missionary."

I suppose I should have challenged her more strongly. But already I felt compromised, complicit. I might so easily have killed him myself.

"When are you leaving the country?" Grace asked.

"Tomorrow morning. So it's goodbye and God Bless. I've always thought well of you," Muriel said, addressing me directly. "You're a quiet little thing and a good listener" – not exactly an effusive tribute, but I felt touched by it.

Mr Shelley

Mr Shelley

Most people who work here have never even glimpsed Mr Shelley. To them he's just a name on telephone extension lists and company notepaper. JPL Shelley, one of the directors, a member of the founder's family. If only they knew! But perhaps it's best they don't, since people can be so cruel and intolerant.

The Alfred Marks recruitment consultant was dressed in shocking pink and wore black-rimmed glasses. "I'm sorry, we've got nothing for you," she told me. "Frankly, I'm surprised you even bothered to apply with typing skills like these" – she was staring disbelievingly at the results of my test. "An employer would really have to be desperate – oh, wait a minute!" she called me back from the door. "We do have *one* client..."

Mrs Box, the personnel manager at Shelley Lingham Green, looked kind but worn-out, like my old English teacher. She didn't ask me many questions and those she did ask were peculiar ones – for instance, was I repelled by any particular common or garden creature? Did I eat French food?

It began to sound like she was interviewing me for a different kind of job altogether. "Excuse me," I said. "Shelley

Lingham Green are building contractors, aren't they?"

"The second-largest in the UK and number five in the world!" she confirmed.

"And I would be working here as a secretary?"

"Yes, of course. Now if you'll just sign this form. It's our standard confidentiality agreement..."

We went up two floors in the lift, to level seven. Our heels clacked down empty corridors. No hum of computers or buzz of conversation, not even any coffee machines. Mr Shelley must be a private sort of person, I thought, or a lonely one. And here was I, chosen to share his solitude.

"I'll leave you here," she whispered at the open door to Mr Shelley's room, which looked more like a greenhouse than an office.

"It's best you should go in alone. You're not nervous, are you? He's awfully nice, really. Don't let appearances deceive you."

I made my way cautiously into the room, through interlacing fern fronds and then a curtain of hanging vines. The first thing I saw, once my eyes adjusted to the gloom, was a snail as big as an armchair. Mr Shelley was obviously a wildlife enthusiast. What next, a tarantula?

"Mr Shelley!" I called tremulously, expecting him to emerge from some other part of the office.

But instead the snail replied, "Yes, that's me." The voice was cultivated, precise.

"I'm your new secretary," I said, feeling a bit stunned.

"Good. Delighted to meet you, Miss..."

"Amanda."

"James." And he smiled – a nice smile, though toothless – and his horns moved back and forth in greeting signals.

I won't say I wasn't scared at first. It took me a long time to get used to him. Imagine working in a small office with someone like that – a wild creature really, who even if he didn't have savage instincts, might kill or hurt me just by accident. For instance, what if I got trapped in his path and he ran over me, engulfing me in all that suffocating squidginess? But at least he didn't move fast. That was one comfort.

And he was very patient, unlike most human beings. My shorthand really wasn't up to much, so he would dictate slowly, while I sat typing at the computer. Then he would examine the screen and correct my spelling. In a kind way, not making me feel stupid. "I think you may be dyslexic," he told me. "I'm surprised they didn't pick it up at your school."

January passed and February. I rearranged Mr Shelley's filing system. He was a nice boss to work for – he made me feel like quite a good secretary and that boosted my confidence. I told him things about my family – my sister and her kids, my dad – that I'd never discussed with anyone.

Then it was my birthday, March the fourteenth. I was 21 years old. "Ta-rah!" Mr Shelley cried.

Red roses in a vase on my desk. A bottle of champagne. A huge box of Belgian chocolates.

"Oh James, how did you know? You shouldn't have gone to all this trouble for me."

He was beaming – and if you think a snail can't beam, you're quite wrong. We drank the champagne from beautiful wide glasses, tinted with elusive, darting, rainbow colours. They weren't proper champagne glasses, but more convenient for Mr Shelley than the long, narrow type. I set his glass on the floor and he sipped from it. He made a joke about beer traps – for slugs – which seemed very amusing at the time.

Still drunk when I got home, I stumbled over a toy truck left in the hall corridor. My sister's children were running up and down, screaming hysterically. "Dad wants to speak to you. He's in the sitting-room," she told me.

I wasn't expecting my father to be there. He keeps irregular hours and we often don't see him for weeks on end. He's always up to something and it's usually – well, not criminal, but not exactly legal either. He's a professional photographer. He used to be a handsome man and you can still see it – the lean, tanned face, now hung around with greasy grey hair, the wolfish smile. He's very thin, from drinking and not eating.

"Laur tells me you've landed a good job, working for a top dog?"

"Not a dog" – then I started giggling and couldn't stop. My working for a snail seemed very funny, all of a sudden. I'd never seen the humour in the situation before.

And then I told him. Of course he was the worst person I could possibly have chosen. Other people's secrets are meat and drink to him.

He seemed doubtful at first. "It sounds like the Elephant Man – some kind of deformity?"

"Oh no, Dad. He's really, really a snail." Even as I insisted, my heart began beating hard with dread. But it was too late. He went on questioning me, until at last I revealed the weak point in Mr Shelley's defences.

Behind the office building was a garden, surrounded by its own high walls, where Mr Shelley lived outside working hours. He reached it by sliding down the outside wall of the building. Sometimes we'd taken walks there together.

My father drove me back to the office. "Now here's what I want you to do, Mandy..."

I took his camera and hid it under my coat. I told myself, I'm not stealing anything, only pictures. The security guard smiled at me as I passed his little glass cabin. Soon I was inside the walled garden.

I hid behind a bush and waited until he appeared on top of the garden wall. And how gorgeous he looked, with all the colours of his shell brought out by the rain!

As he was coming down, I took the first picture. The camera flash startled him – he shrank into his shell. "Who's there?" he called from inside.

Click, flash. Click, flash.

"Who is it? Why are you doing this?"

Then I burst into tears and ran – out from the garden, away from all familiar landmarks, down streets I didn't know. Dark blots on the wet pavement – snails tempted out by the rain, harmless creatures, Mr Shelley's miniature brothers and sisters. And they crunched under my shoes, I couldn't avoid them, and they lay broken, leaking out their life fluid. And then I smashed the camera open and pulled out its ribbons of film, like intestines. A butcher, me, a murderer.

"Thank God you're back!" Mrs Box greeted me a week later. That surprised me. I'd expected her to spit in my face. But she obviously knew nothing. Mr Shelley must not have told her how I'd betrayed him.

"I've come to collect my P45."

"Why? Why, Mandy? What's happened?"

"I can't explain," I said. "I'm sorry, it's a personal matter. You can hire another secretary."

"But he's dying!" Mrs Box clapped a hand to her mouth. I noticed her eyes were bloodshot, her hair untidy.

"Dying?" I whispered.

"He won't let anyone into his room, even the cleaners. And he hasn't eaten for a week. I'm so worried about him. Please, please…"

"All right, I'll go up there," I said unwillingly. "He probably won't let me in either."

"Bless you, Mandy. You don't look too well yourself."

"I'm all right." But of course I was in a dreadful state, having been crying all week. I'd come to the shocking realisation, Mr Shelley meant more to me than all my family put together. A snail, my soulmate.

The delicate fronds at the entrance to Mr Shelley's office were brown and drooping. The curtain of vines had become thickly matted, so I had to tear my way through. The first thing I saw was the champagne bottle, still on my desk, a quarter full, and our empty glasses, with all the rainbow lights vanished from them. I didn't see Mr Shelley at first, until he spoke.

"It was you, wasn't it?"

His shell all dull and dirty. And that shocked me – he was usually so meticulous, insistent on things being kept hygienic. Then I realised, the stickiness under my feet was his trail, which the cleaners usually removed every night.

"Yes. It was me."

"I expect your father put you up to it." Mr Shelley said nothing for a while. Then he sighed. "Well, we all make mistakes."

"But I betrayed your secret!"

"It was bound to happen some time or another."

"Please, Mr Shelley, stop making excuses for me. I don't deserve your forgiveness and it's just making me feel even worse."

"I've been thinking about your father," he said, unexpectedly. "About him and the Loch Ness monster."

When my dad was young, he spent months camping by Loch Ness, hoping to catch a glimpse of the monster. He didn't want to sell pictures of it, unlikely as it may seem. He just wanted to see it.

Mr Shelley said, "Of course, it's sad to be a monster oneself and to be forced to hide from prying eyes. But it's sadder to lose your sense of wonder."

"You see so much, Mr Shelley," I said. "Do you see anything in me?"

"A great capacity for love."

Not quite daring to reveal my feelings, I asked him, "Who can I love?"

"That's not for me to say."

I took some tissues, moistened them with champagne and started gently wiping the dirt and dust from his shell.

This is written years afterwards. At the point I was describing, Mr Shelley turned from a snail back into a man. For he'd been put under a spell that could only be broken by someone falling in love with him – someone loving him for who he was and for no other reason.

As a young man he'd been promoted very fast, owing to family connections. This of course aroused bad feeling. One person engaged the services of a necromancer, then slipped a potion into James's coffee. See how it feels, being in the slow lane…

Sometimes in my memory the shell cracks all over, sometimes it dissolves away gradually as I'm wiping it with the tissues. Perhaps that was the last twist of the enchantment, casting a veil of confusion over its own workings.

We got married six months later and I wish we hadn't invited my father to the wedding, his behaviour was a disgrace. I left my job, there being no need for me to carry on working.

The walled garden was destroyed by bulldozers. I did regret that, but felt I hadn't any right to complain, living in a mock-Tudor house in Surrey with all the garden I could desire. James has done very well. He's got a new super-efficient secretary, to match his new fast-paced ways. Even at home he can't relax – he's always on the phone or dictating letters or sending e-mails. Compared with him I often feel slow and stupid.

Other women envy me the big house, money in the bank, foreign holidays. But these are not what I fell in love with. They're not what I really want. And James – well. He seems to have turned into someone I don't even like that much.

Lupercal

Lupercal

Beware, his mind told him, of people who have in the course of their lives neither taken part in an orgy nor gone through the experience of childbirth, for they are dangerous people...

Isak Dinesen, *Seven Gothic Tales*

The arrival of wolves in Stoke Newington, a fashionable area of north-east London, did not at first cause widespread panic, or even much concern. Although some people worried about house prices, a general stagnancy in the property market made it difficult to judge if these were affected. Also, Stoke Newington is full of psychotherapists, who refused to believe in the wolves as objective reality, doubting even the evidence of their own eyes. Thus lycantherapy developed, a complex science, and many profound theses and articles were written. My friend Alice, who was training to be a child psychotherapist, presented a special paper to the Tavistock Clinic: "Wolves in our Waking Dreams: a study of mass paranoia in Stoke Newington".

I congratulated myself secretly on living in Tottenham, next to a nice park with no wolves in it. Alice lives near Abney Park

Cemetery, a hauntingly atmospheric place, with its fallen tomb-stones overgrown with ivy, its family graves and those of possible lovers, a war memorial commemorating whole streets of people, a stone lion outstretched on its keeper's grave and the stone angels, some with human faces. Here the wolves congregated and might easily be observed, padding in and out of the ruined chapel, peering around gravestones, playing with their cubs in patches of sunlight. Here, while walking one day with Alice, I kissed her on the mouth and she let me, and our kissing continued for a long, sweet, seemingly endless moment. Then she said, "Don't do that. Ever again."

A grey wolf crossed our path some way ahead, emerging on one side from the brambled undergrowth, delicately negotiating a puddle. "Look, there's a wolf," I said, pointing. "Quick, look – you can still see its tail. Oh, it's gone..."

Soon after that day, Alice acquired a boyfriend called R. He owned an antique shop in Islington. She had some doubts about his intelligence. Alice placed intelligence high on her list of priorities for a boyfriend. She was choosing the father of her child as well as her own life partner. I've never known anyone so serious as Alice about choices, about life. A childless woman approaching forty, she felt responsibilities towards herself. I was twenty-nine and terminally indecisive – devoured by longings, by sexual hunger, by romantic dreams. After Alice found R, I got no more kisses from her. A man, however unsatisfactory, was what she wanted.

This was a lonely time. I used to sit in the cemetery and watch the wolves. Sometimes I talked out loud to them. Their faces looked so intelligent, I was sure they understood me. I fed them with bread and biscuits and cake. They liked Mr Kipling best.

I knew there was something strange about R. Alice never suspected – which just shows how unreliable sex is as the touchstone of anyone's nature. Contrary to popular lore and fairy stories, we preserve our disguises even in bed. Especially men do, because they seldom have souls, true selves to be revealed. I uncovered R's secret while exploring my own fearful desires. When I was a little girl I had nightmares about wolves, of being eaten by a wolf.

The wolfskin

There was a woman, she lived around here, a long time ago. She had no husband, no pretty little children, no lover, no dear friends, not even a dog or a cat, nothing. She fancied a man, but he was married to someone else. So the woman went to visit her great-aunt, her only living relation, who was a witch. She lived in Somerleyton, in Suffolk, with some other witches, in a witch community.

"Tell me, Great-aunt, how to ensnare the man I love."

"Puf!" replied the old woman. "Take my advice and leave me alone. He'll be a pain in the arse and a grief to your heart."

But the woman persisted, "I must have this man."

Grumbling and mumbling her toothless jaws, the old woman went to the chest where she kept all her magic things, including the skins and mummified paws of many different animals. She gave the woman a wolfskin. "At the full moon, put on this wolfskin. The man will fall in love with you, against his will and good judgement, he will not reject your advances, he will sleep with you and give you a child."

The woman took the wolfskin and went back home. She waited until the full moon. Then she put on the wolfskin. Except for her breasts, her belly and the parts below, she looked just like a wolf.

Even her nails grew into sharp wolf claws and her eyes had a green wolfish glint. She broke into the man's house through a downstairs window. His old mother and father were sitting on a bench by the fireplace. The wolf-woman killed them both, she ate their flesh, she drank their blood, she crunched up their bones. Then she crept upstairs. In the first bedroom she found a baby and a small child. She ate the baby. The small child woke up. She ate the small child. In the next bedroom, she found the man, lying asleep with his wife beside him. She ate the wife and she lay down beside the man. "Wake up, dear husband," she whispered. "I am ready for you now. Come into me, fill me."

The man woke, they made love. It was dark in the room. "Dear wife, how fierce you are tonight. What sharp teeth you have. Draw back the shutters and let me see you. As we are married, we need not be ashamed or fearful of our nakedness."

"No, husband, I prefer to make love in the dark."

After a bit the man fell asleep and snored. The wolf-woman lay awake feeling hungry and disappointed. "He was not worth it," she said to herself. "Next time, I shall find myself a real wolf."

R's antique shop, the Gothic Castle, is situated just off Upper Street. He specialises in Victorian birdcages and fish tanks. Also dusty plastic flowers arranged in cracked vases, stuffed pheasants and mousetraps.

He could never remember my name. Or did he deliberately forget? He disliked most of Alice's friends and acquaintances, all those pre-dating their relationship. He felt "threatened", as she explained, "judged" by us. It's true that I thought him a stupid nerd, undeserving of anyone so special and clever as Alice. But that was before I grew suspicious.

Chopin's Nocturnes were playing scratchily on one of those 1920s gramophone players with a silver tube for a record arm. R was slumped in an armchair by the till, reading the *Islington Gazette*. He wore a striped knitted tanktop over an unbuttoned and torn shirt. "Sorry, closed," he said, not looking up.

"It's Jane," I said loudly. "Alice's friend."

"Oh, er." He blinked at me "Can I...?"

"You're a werewolf," I said. "Don't trouble to deny it." I took a gun out of my bag and pointed it at him. It was plastic, but looked convincing. My hands were shaking.

"Don't shoot," he said, faintly ironic.

Soon after, rummaging in the second-hand bookshop below Vortex on Church Street, I found a book I had given Alice, with both our names written on the flyleaf, scored out.

I didn't just lose Alice, I lost all my friends. I lost them one after the other, with careful violent intention. Like shooting pigeons out of the sky. I said the worst things I'd ever thought of saying. I wrote poisonous letters. I laughed a lot, for no apparent reason. I was sacked from my job. I offended even distant acquaintances and passers-by. I beat a man up in the tube, on the Piccadilly line between Arnos Grove and Southgate. I stole things from shops. I talked wildly and used foul language. I even made my mother cry.

One night I cut off most of my hair and it flew away in the sky, twittering like a flock of starlings. The rest fell out. I was seeing doctors. They injected me, they loaded me down. My body went numb, especially my hands and arms and in a circle around my mouth. My eyes itched, they were bleeding poison.

The problem was, I let too much power flood into me at once. You see, I didn't realise, women are different from men.

We don't split so easily and cleanly down the middle. We turn into monsters. The wolf entered me, I became the wolf.

In the wasteland, in litter-strewn, desolate streets, past McDonald's, around Dalston Junction, through Ridley Road Market walks the lone and hungry wolf. Oh She-wolf, divine Wolf-bitch, Mother of Wolves, Lupa, transform your votaries into your likeness. By the new moon, under the full moon, in the moon's changes we arise and howl (*collective howl*). Your red-hooded girls, your sweet-fleshed victims, we call on you, oh Mother (*howl repeated*).

– Part of an ancient charm, updated for present-day use, to be spoken by women wishing to invoke the Moon goddess and become werewolves.

"Please," he said, stretching out his hand. "Give me the gun."

"Stay where you are!" I shouted.

He stopped in front of me. There was a powerful smell of wolf – a hot sharp stink. Sex or fear. Coming from one of us. He was still in human form, but I feared at any second he might turn.

He touched my face. His finger left a numb spot. "I'm just a man," he said. "Normal and fairly harmless."

I let the gun drop. I wanted his tongue inside my mouth. "You're an interesting kind of girl," he said. "You hold a lot back, don't you?"

The Bulking Store

The Bulking Store

Fresh and salt water mingle here, though to taste it's bitter salt, the river water drowned. See those four narrow granite slabs set in the quay, by the camomile lawn? What are they, what might they conceal? Can you guess? *She* doesn't like them, although ignorant of the reason; I've seen her glance at them uneasily. But she likes watching the cormorant perched on a white dinghy, its wings forever outstretched to dry. The baby is asleep in her arms and soon she nods off too, lulled by the clinking of halyards against hollow aluminium masts, the hushing of small waves.

They've taken the coastguard's cottage for a fortnight. She's alone with her children for the first week. "Bye, Mum! We're going up the beach," her boys cry. Then rushing back with some trophy – shells, a crab in a bucket. "We saw a seal!"

"A seal? Really?" Tucking a wisp of hair into its plait. Cuddling her little girl.

They go on a picnic, taking the ferry to Old Cellars beach from the landing stage outside the hotel. A pound each. I go along too, no extra charge. Peter the ferryman steers the outboard motor while gazing into the distance, future or past. His hair is sleeked back under a cap, his skin is smooth. On the home journey, just us two in the boat, he asks, "Why are you still hanging around here?"

"I might ask the same question of you, my friend."

"Oh, I'm the landlubber now. Married a woman who took my fancy and we've got two kids. So I've broken off communications with my side of the family and stuff my ears with wax at night so I won't hear them...you know..."

"Where's your coat?"

"In storage." He'd never tell me or anyone else where – the old superstition – but of course it's not destroyed. One day his wife will be tidying out a cupboard and she'll ask him "Pete, what's this manky old thing?" Then he'll be off again.

"The past is what traps you," he says. "I mean, keeps you from leaving this place."

"Traps is the right word."

"You could be free as the sea foam. As light on water."

"And as easily dispersed. Wind would scatter me then, a cloud expunge me. I fear being at the mercy of the universe. It's OK for you – a live thing still, though changeable."

"Where are your bones?" he asks. "Still in that old tank at the Bulking Store? Or did they give you a decent burial – in the churchyard, maybe?" The little church stands high on the hill above the creek, separated by a few untidy layers of cottages from the Swan pub, where they do a nice crab salad. Sit on a bench with your pint of cider and bask here – it's a sun-trap. The creek is rich mud, stalked by gulls and oyster catchers. You'd think the sea had lost interest in this little corner, but no, look at the tide rippling over the Voss, a walkway across the mud. There's already enough water to float a few ducks and soon your boat.

"Where are my bones? That's a bit of a personal question." My laughter sounds like a gull's cry. I'm not bitter. The men who dumped me in that tank – yes, below the granite slabs, where they used to store shellfish before taking them up to sell at Plymouth – those men are long dead. Long dead.

That night after putting her children to bed she seems to be waiting, listening for something – a call from her husband, maybe? Or maybe not. Anyway the phone doesn't ring. She writes a couple of postcards, then examines the bookcase. Dick Francis, Catherine Cookson, the usual holiday cottage selection. One book looks different and she pulls it out: a blue, leatherbound collection of poems. I'd guess she hasn't read any poetry since school.

"Mummy!" Her younger lad is standing in the doorway. "The sea came up higher and higher and then we had to swim and I couldn't so I was frightened and you carried me but then we all drowned..."

"Darling, it was only a dream. Back to bed now..." Alone, I reflect on her unhappiness. Something's wrong in her marriage. That's not a guess, I can feel it. Opening a little space for me, the first opportunity I've had in a while. Meanwhile, I wait to hear a cradlesong, a lullaby – ah no, mothers don't sing their children to sleep any more. Those old ways are vanished from the world, among so many other lovely things. A breeze from the French windows riffles the pages of her book. I blow to help them turn, until a poem I like appears, one I want her to read. *The Forsaken Merman*.

Come, dear children, let us away;
Down and away below!
Now my brothers call from the bay,
Now the great winds shoreward blow,
Now the salt tides seaward flow...

You know it? The story of a mortal woman who married a merman, but then went back to her home village; the narrow paved streets, the little grey church on the windy hill. Now her sea-husband and merchildren cry out for her to return, yearn for her. It's a poem of the sea and of longing. The two go together.

I feel unusually strong. If not substantial, at least gathering substance. Almost alive – but of course it's not my own life, it's something taken from her. I've been hungry for this, like an anemone waiting for its pool to flood with new life, with prey. Or a limpet clinging to the rock, enduring the dry time.

She puts the anthology back in the bookcase without glancing inside. Never mind. I'm wondering, could I slip into her dreams – extend a delicate, questing tentacle further into her mind/heart?

She leans on the balcony; gazes at the glittering path of moonlight on dark water. Out there, in the sea, I'd be so much more powerful. Could I induce her to go swimming? No, I'm afraid – unwilling to mingle my spirit with hers. It would feel like drowning...

Next day he appears out of a bright mist. He hops from the boat, ignoring Peter's ridged landing plank. The boys scramble on board – today they're going to sailing school. Waving goodbye, smiling, she tells our unexpected visitor: "You shouldn't be here."

"I just wanted to see you." Dumps his sports bag on the quay. "I've booked myself in at the hotel. If anyone asks, pretend I'm your husband."

"And when Joe turns up next week?"

"Say he's your lover. Well, hello there..." He tickles the baby, who laughs flirtatiously. Two easily won females. And meanwhile I fade...

They sit dangling their legs over the quayside, his arm around her waist. The baby's been put down for her nap. Lovers in the sun. Kisses, murmurs. "Do you love me? And will you always..." You know the sort of thing. Timeless babble. She threads daisies above my tomb. She doesn't care now, intuits nothing, senses nothing. Because she's happy.

Oh, I'm weak again, drawn back – back into the dark and filthy tank. Untangling me from the net they tumbled me in, then crowbarred the slabs into position, trapping me in that sea dungeon. First seal, then man, I grasped at iron rungs set in the concrete, pulling myself up to where I could see a chink of light – then fell, hitting my head. And as a man I drowned...

"Let's go for a swim!"

Yes, let's. I slip into the water after them. He swims far out, showing off, while she admires from the shallows. I'm with him, encouraging. Further! Further! The sun dazzles; she shades her eyes. Is that him, or a buoy? Or a seal? Meantime, he's in trouble. Cramp seizes him. He struggles and chokes. I'm there, sucking the air from his lungs. It takes no time at all. So easy...

Is it possible for a man to drown and then come back to life? It is – although of course the "he" who returns may not be precisely the same person. But if the body's inhabiter is skilful, no one will notice.

"I couldn't see you! I was afraid you'd drowned!"

"No, my darling..."

The child is fretful after her nap and won't smile at me. Turns her face into her mother's neck. And when we're kissing, she tries with all her baby strength to push me away...

Our Sweetness and Our Hope

Our Sweetness and Our Hope

The ocean at night swallows up every light. Even the moon's beams are sucked in. The water is dead cold. I am going into it very slowly, feet first, letting it creep up me, a prolonged unbearable shudder. The waves nibble at me like tiny fish.

I have a terrible deep wound in me somewhere. Go into the sea, she said, let the salt water heal you. I'm swimming now, carrying myself swiftly out in the darkness. Hanging on the surface, depths unfolding below me, where huge things move silently. Sharks. Big mouths full of teeth, razor-sharp, white, lethal. They could shear off an arm or a leg so casually it would feel just like a passing bump, a nudge. Or half my body gone. Just like that.

A joke. I hate practical jokes. I'd rather see it coming to me, glimpse the teeth before I'm inside the shark. Which parts of me will it spit out again, which parts savour as delicacies?

Nothing breaks surface or betrays itself by so much as a ripple. Darkness and utter silence. I put my face down in the water, open my eyes forcibly and look. The light instantly dazzles me, glorious underwater golden-green light. The sharks – three sharks, four – are drifting contentedly in the golden depths.

Then the light goes off. I'm jolted awake. We've reached the terminus, the bus garage. I've travelled by night bus all the way from Trafalgar Square. The impatient driver is flicking his lights on and off, to encourage my departure. I put my book away – it is *Jaws*, the original paperback by Peter Benchley. A young woman flitters up from the back seat, like a startled moth. She looks exceedingly pale, bloodless, drained. Perhaps it's just the light.

This was my first meeting with Selina. The dream introduced her to me, contained and presented in neat metaphor all the most important elements of our future relationship: blood, danger, a hidden enemy, unexpected reversals of light and darkness, fear and attraction – all suggested themselves, without a word spoken.

Song of the Vampire (anon – a translation)
I am too full of blood tonight
The moon's white face is masked in a veil of blood
Blood drips from her, like tears
I am flesh made by the moon, my lady mother and
   cruel mistress...

Selina explained vaguely that she came from "outside London". Her voice was curiously lacking in timbre, but with a harsh, grating accent. Of course, it never occurred to me that she was a vampire. Otherwise I might have thought twice about inviting her back to my flat.

She was remarkably colourless; not so much pale as emptied of colour, bleached dry, like bone. She conveyed the effect of a negative photograph, something one stage removed from real. She was like a vacuum, everything disappeared into her. Words, thoughts. I chattered inanely as we walked along the pavement, she smiled and said nothing. I wondered why I was putting myself out so, for a stranger. But she had this attractive quality – of being fictional, obviously not true, a character from a story or legend.

And since I have already let slip that she was a vampire, you may be curious to know what happened between us. Whether she bit me and whether – since yes, she did, and obviously I survived the experience – she then allowed me the opportunity of biting her, and if so, whether I proceeded with due caution, keeping in mind (a) the peril of my immortal soul and (b) the HIV virus and the danger of its transference through exchange of blood, not to speak of Hepatitis B.

Not until many moons later did Selina draw blood from me, and then only with the greatest reluctance. The reason for her translucent paleness, on our first meeting, was that she had given up vampirism. She had gone to the opposite extreme, or perhaps not, of becoming a Roman Catholic. She wore a cross around her neck. She thought it would protect her, from other vampires perhaps, or from herself.

She confided shyly in me that she was taking instruction at the Roman Catholic church at Southgate. Now I have a horror of Catholicism, having myself, like a remarkable number of other lesbians, been brought up in the faith. I am still not free of that legacy of years. "Catholics!" I exclaimed, with an indrawn hiss. "I should steer well clear of them, if I were you. Unless you enjoy sadomasochism in the name of love."

We stood together under the orange streetlamp, below my flat. I wondered, should I invite her up for coffee? Her eyes were silver-grey, enormous in the strange light.

"It's my family," she said simply. "The problem is my family."

"Oh?"

"My mother in particular. She doesn't like me associating with common mortals. What she calls 'mixing it'."

"Who else are you supposed to associate with? Immortals?" I laughed.

"Immortals, yes."

"Your mother sounds a bit odd."

"She is…" Selina hesitated. "She only drinks every couple of years. But then she really goes for it."

"On a pub crawl?"

"A trail of bloodless corpses."

I presumed bloodless corpses was slang for empty glasses or bottles. So the old lady was an alcoholic. "But your mother isn't here now."

Selina glanced round nervously. Something fluttered beyond the circle of light – a bat or a moth. "She still snoops on me. Excuse me." Selina turned. "Fuck off, fuck off!" she screeched into the darkness.

I saw something run like a huge spider, graceful and swift, up the vertical sidewall of my neighbour's house. "Excuse me," Selina said again. "We had better go indoors. I think I will, after all, take up your kind offer of a bed for the night."

I could not recall having made any such kind offer. But I was too tired to argue.

I made Selina up a bed in the sitting room. She was asleep when I left for work the next morning. And when I came back from work, there she was, still fast asleep.

Her silver-ash hair spread around her, falling over the pillows to the floor. It looked as though she was lying in a pool of metal. Maybe that would account, I thought, for the pallor of her skin, her air of exhaustion. The hair was draining all her strength.

It is my evening custom to smoke a cigarette on the balcony outside my bedroom window. The balcony is about two yards by one yard, enough to accommodate one deckchair and one potted plant. It is structurally unsound, as the surveyor informed me when I moved into the flat ten years ago; also the floor is rotten and likely to collapse at any moment, in which case I should plunge to a certain death. This adds a pleasant spice of danger to my evening ritual. I smoke Silk Cut, having been seduced by the subliminally violent advertisements, eg the chainsaw wrapped up in purple silk.

The sun slipped behind the industrial estate. I was just stubbing out my cigarette when Selina appeared. She wore an old-fashioned black dress, high necked, with long, tight sleeves ending in black frills at the wrists. "That's an addiction," she said, pointing at the ashtray in my lap.

"It's an addiction I happen to enjoy."

"You'll taste horrible."

"Smoking has certainly affected my sense of taste – I suppose it's the" – my voice faltered – "sorry, what did you just say?"

Selina leant against the window frame, looking pale and elegant. I noticed she had very long, white fingers and toes. Her bare feet seemed extraordinarily narrow. I wondered fleetingly how she ever got shoes to fit them. "Where I come from, people are judged like wines, in terms of their purity and 'body'. A strong taint of tobacco can be ruinous. I don't think you'd appeal to connoisseurs like my sister Ludmilla, for instance, but then Ludmilla has an exceptionally discriminating palate. She can scarcely drink anything stronger than the fresh blood of a tender newborn babe... it's very difficult for her. Newborn babes are so well guarded nowadays, even against common baby snatchers, let alone vampires. It was different a couple of centuries back, when baby girls would frequently be exposed and left to die on the hillsides – then Ludmilla had a wonderful time."

"I expect she did. So your sister is a vampire?" I coughed over the word.

"Yes. We all are, all seven of us."

"Good heavens."

"But I'm trying to change." Selina anxiously twisted her long fingers together. "It limits one's social life dreadfully. You're just starting to get to know someone interesting, then it's so tempting to bite them, and then of course they die – or become vampires. So boring. I want to broaden my horizons. I think it's happening already. I'm really beginning to *appreciate* people – not just how they taste, but for themselves."

"If you want to broaden your horizons, I would forget about Catholicism."

"Oh, but the priest – he's so nice. Father Michael. He helped me to stop drinking."

I remembered the bloodless corpses. "Don't you, er, drink at all nowadays?"

"Strawberry milkshake," Selina said solemnly. "Nothing else."

"My dear girl. Does it provide you with the right nutrients?"

"No, but it's good for my soul."

"How charming," I said, with a touch of condescension, thinking how sweet and naive she was. Those godawful Catholics. "I didn't think vampires had souls."

Selina turned even paler than before, literally white at the lips. Her fingernails, I noticed, were clear as glass. "By God's grace," she said, "I'll receive one tomorrow, when I'm baptised."

The next day was Sunday and Selina's baptism was scheduled for three o'clock. I drove her to the church, feeling it was the least I could do in the circumstances – she was by now in a state of teeth-chattering terror. There was hardly any traffic, until we stopped at some lights; then I glimpsed a big black car, like a hearse, pulling out of a side road. I looked in the driving mirror. There was the car, behind us, but it seemed to be empty. I re-marked on this to Selina, who glanced over her shoulder. "Oh my God!" she shrieked. "It's my family! Drive on, drive on!"

I could not resist looking round, which was a bad mistake. The hearse, I could now see, contained seven women dressed in black. Selina's mother sat in the front passenger seat, distinguished by her thin, aristocratic nose and glittering eyes. The chauffeur, un-derneath his peaked cap, was obviously dead, and rapidly decom-posing.

The lights changed and I slammed my foot down on the accel-erator – luckily I knew an alternative route and we arrived at the church on time.

Agremina

Selina told me this story, of her love affair with a mortal woman:

I've sucked blood from countless numbers of women. Some died, some survived. But I've only been in love once. Her name was Agremina and she lived in the nineteenth century, in rural Transylvania. I met her outside the town alehouse, late one night – she was waiting for her father, who often needed help getting home. I was just waiting – you know – for anyone who might come stumbling out of the alehouse door. Drunkards are easy prey, even if they taste foul. We got talking and I told her I was a vampire. She wasn't afraid. We talked about – oh, all kinds of things. Especially books. We had the same tastes in literature, it turned out; she liked Emily Dickinson too. And we both loved walking in the mountains.

It felt as though we'd known each other all our lives. She was so beautiful and so good, I fell in love with her. And she felt the same way about me. She told me so. "You don't mind me being a vampire, then?" I said anxiously.

"Oh Selina, I don't think of you as a vampire."

Well, in the early days that was enough, she made me happy, and the kissing and so on was lovely, but then increasingly I began to feel terribly frustrated. The wanting to bite feeling – it became awfully strong.

So I wrote her a letter, a farewell letter, saying it was best we should part, although I still loved her desperately. After I'd sent the letter I heard nothing from her for a week or more. I stayed in the castle, pacing up and down my room, in agony and torment. One night, when the moon was full, I went up on the castle battlements, and through the trees I glimpsed my mother's carriage – that was before she got a car – bowling at a fast pace down the long winding road to the town.

Instantly I was seized with a dread suspicion. Throwing my cloak around me, I sped downstairs to the shed where I kept my rusty old black bicycle, and was soon in desperate pursuit. But it was too late. When I reached the town my mother's carriage was nowhere to be seen. I went straight to Agremina's house. It was plunged in darkness. I climbed through her bedroom window and managed to light a candle. She was lying on the bed, deathly pale. She only just had enough strength left to gasp a few words.

She had written a letter, saying that she loved me, that she would give me – everything, that she would be waiting for me that night. My mother had intercepted the letter and – you can guess the rest.

I bit into my wrist and held it to Agremina's lips. I begged her on my knees to drink – to drink my own heart's blood, to live forever – but she was too weak by then. She turned her face away from me and died.

Now can you wonder that I hold my mother in such hatred?

While Selina was being baptised, I sat chain-smoking in the car outside. Not long after our arrival I saw the hearse slide up the road like a crocodile and park by the cemetery gates. Selina's sisters emerged and clambered over the wall, with the ungainly groping movements of night creatures in sunlight. Her mother and the deceased chauffeur remained inside the car. Although she never once looked in my direction, I'm sure she knew I was there.

Through the cemetery gates I could see Selina's sisters dancing round the gravestones, their black garments flapping. The clock on the church tower showed 3.15 and as its two hands joined in a single pointing arrow, I heard an unearthly scream from the church. The sisters went into a huddle – the collective noun for vampires. I felt convinced that Selina was being tortured or even murdered inside the church; indeed baptism has always seemed to me an act of violence, pouring cold water over a screaming innocent child, wrenching the devil out of her. And with a poor vampire, presumably forcing the "soul" in. Any spare soul the priest happens to have lying around in the vestry, inside some dusty cupboard?

I wrenched open the car door and hurried up the path towards the church. Selina's sisters came bounding over the graves towards me, waving their arms, but just in time I slipped inside the porch.

Not pausing to read the notices about cleaning rotas and pilgrimages, I entered the darkened church. Furious whisperings could be heard up by the font; stealing behind a pillar, I saw a hatted woman proffering a first-aid kit. The priest was fumbling with a tube of Savlon. Selina was looking terrified and guilty, with wet hair. I beckoned frantically at her and she hurried towards me, trembling.

"I bit him," she whispered.

"You bit the priest?"

"When he poured the holy water on me – it scalded my skin like fire. I couldn't help – it wasn't really a bite. I just sort of grazed him."

"Oh dear, Selina."

"You're a very ungrateful young lady!" exclaimed the hatted woman. "Look what you've done to poor Father Michael. You'll need a tetanus injection for that, Father." And she urged him solicitously away into the vestry.

"Let's go," Selina said, on the verge of tears.

"Your sisters have got the church surrounded."

"I'll fight my way out."

"You're not strong enough, dear. They've fed well recently, n the look of them." I was surprised how easily this affection-
ithet rose to my lips. It was the first time I had called any-
ar for ten years or more.

wept tears of blood. They stained her dress and left un-
g red streaks on her skin. "Oh, Joanna, I'm so sorry I got
s mess. If only I'd been more careful."

a rustling movement among the darkened pews.
nside her dress and held up the crucifix. I looked
weapon. My eye fell on some spiky black iron

candlesticks beneath a statue of Our Lady. But before I could seize these, a young woman emerged from the shadows. She was dark-skinned, with long black hair, and she was carrying a baby in one arm while arranging her dress; she'd been breastfeeding. "I can help you," she said gently to Selina. "If you'll just hold the baby for me, please…"

Selina obeyed with alacrity. The baby waved its arms in her face and gurgled. "Oh, what a darling – choo choo," she murmured.

The young woman hurried back, swinging a brass ball on three chains. "This is used for asperges," she said. "For sprinkling holy water over the congregation. Gather the chains low down and you can direct the water accurately through these little holes. It won't hurt you," she said, addressing Selina. "That was only your fear. Holy water never harmed anyone. But it will vanquish your enemies, joined with my prayers for your safety. Hurry now!" and she took the baby back.

"But are we allowed…?" Selina protested at the door. "The priest …won't he…?"

The woman smiled. "I say what's allowed," she said. "It's my church. Light a candle to me next time you come here."

Selina's sisters made a concerted lunge as we emerged, but the holy water ball got us through safely.

Vampire bat

A famous naturalist, on an expedition to collect rare species for his open-air zoo in the Channel Islands, determined to capture a vampire bat. He was travelling in a mountainous district of South America, when he stopped to ask directions from an indigenous hillside farmer, scraping his precarious existence from the rocky terrain. The natural-ist casually raised the subject of vampire bats. Yes, the farmer knew of such creatures. Occasionally, they took blood from his cattle. They had also been known to prey on sleeping human beings. Their sharp teeth made only a small slit in the skin, through which they sucked nourishment, leaving the victim greatly weakened.

Encouraged by this information, the naturalist decided to use himself as bait. He built a high lookout post, and there he slept naked in the moonlight. But the vampire bat never came. Vampire bats are shy creatures, in habit finicky and particular. The natural-ist was forced at last to admit failure and went away despondent. Months afterwards he learnt that the bite of the Argentine blood bat, *Pipistrella sanguinea*, nearly always proves fatal, since the bat's teeth exude a substance that prevents blood from clotting. In the event of success, the naturalist would certainly have bled to death, being ignorant of the antidote, a certain leaf in the forest.

By day Corinne Sanderson (22) works as a legal assistant for a big City firm. Expensive dental treatments have lengthened her upper canines and she avoids garlicky foods. "Since word got around the office, I've not had any problems with sexual harassment," says Corinne. "Vampirism is a fun lifestyle option for young singles."

– "Vamping it up", feature on modern-day vampires in *Lunch Break* magazine.

Little-known facts about vampires

• Vampires hate (vegetable) sugar and all artificial sugary sub-stances. For Selina, drinking strawberry milkshake was a horrible form of self-violence and mortification, equivalent to a human being drinking sewage water.

• A mortal being becomes a vampire on first tasting innocent blood. This may not be for decades. Thereafter, she remains the same age for eternity.

• Sunlight is not harmful to vampires although, being night feeders, they often sleep during the day.

• In type, vampires tend to be thoughtful and sensitive, often artistic.

• They suffer badly from migraines and frequently have nervous breakdowns.

• Virginia Woolf was a vampire. This fact has so far been assiduously concealed by her biographers. But why? It provides an invaluable key to interpretations of her work, eg *Orlando*.

• So was John Donne (*Mark but this flea and mark in this how little that which thou deny'st me is…*)

• No one ever rated normal sex very highly after being bitten by a skilled vampire. The bite imparts an extraordinary pleasure (I can vouch for this myself).

Selina's botched baptism had only one noticeable effect. As if in pity, or by way of compensation for her still-missing reflection/soul, the mirrors in my flat began singing to her. Whenever she looked searchingly, despairingly into, or even just walked past one. Often the air was filled with their beautiful, unearthly high voices.

We still slept in separate beds and I locked my door at night. I wanted her to feel safe. I have never yet trusted my own desires and she stirred depths I would rather not have remembered. Often in passing, in the middle of conversation, when she was laughing, I felt the urge to grab hold of her. But I stopped myself, conscious of being twenty years older, even though she was immortal.

One night we saw a television drama about Karen Carpenter, the talented young singer who died of anorexia. Selina watched the screen intently, leaning forward in her chair. During a moving reconciliation scene between Karen and her mother, several drops of blood rolled down Selina's cheeks. I passed her the box of tissues.

Her decline was rapid, through that autumn and into December. Though death, for her, was not a possibility, she reached that stage. And passed beyond it. During the daytime she looked her age. Several centuries old. At night, given a moon and stars, she appeared again a young girl.

I carried her into my bedroom, where the moon shone directly in at the window. She weighed nothing, it was like holding a skeleton. We lay together on the bed, in the moonlight, in one another's arms, and she told me stories. The mirrors sang softly. The faraway stars chimed like tiny bells.

Then she became unable to speak, even to move her lips. Her eyes turned glassy, empty.

In despair, I returned to the church. The holy water ball was still rattling around in the boot of my car, that was my excuse. My real purpose was to entreat the Virgin for help, to ask for mercy.

She wasn't there. Only the plaster statue. I lit a candle and said a prayer remembered from my childhood:

Hail holy Queen, mother of mercy
Hail our life, our sweetness and our hope
To thee do we cry, poor banished children of Eve

To thee do we send up our sighs, mourning and weeping in
  this vale of tears
Turn then, most gracious advocate, thine eyes of mercy towards us
And after this our exile…

I found myself crying, with the old feeling of not being heard, of praying into a vacuum.

Oh dear Lady, have mercy on Selina. She is innocent, gentle and good. Anyone can see that. So she's a vampire and she may have killed a few people. But that's in her nature, how can you blame her? You understand the need for a drink, don't you, Blessed Virgin? Remember the wedding at Cana, when you turned the water into strong red wine. You have saved the best wine till last, said the amazed guests.

I heard a faint hiss and opened my eyes. A painted green snake was curled around the plaster Virgin's feet; bright-eyed, with shining green scales. The Virgin was obviously fond of it – a favourite pet? – judging by the liberties it was allowed. As I watched, its gold tongue flickered in and out; then it uncurled and slithered away towards the church door.

Though I may be a lapsed Catholic, I can recognise a miraculous sign when I see one. I ran after the snake. Dusk was falling. I followed its metallic green flashing through the churchyard, down the main road, over several crossings, until it vanished into the Moon and Stars pub.

The Virgin Mary was serving behind the crowded bar, pulling pints. She looked harassed, her piled-up hair falling down in wisps. She wore a white T-shirt with a cartoon print; it said "Oh my God, I left the baby on the bus".

I battled my way to the front. When I tried to pay for my lager and lime she said "Forget it. Can't talk right now – see you later. I'm up to my eyeballs with these bastards."

I found a seat near the dartboard. An old lady was playing darts with deadly accuracy, while sipping a Bloody Mary. Selina's mother. Her eyes flickered over me.

"Hello," I said.

"So it's you," she sneered. "The mortal meddler. The half and halfer. The grave worm, that preys on decaying flesh. The sunborn leech, the parasite."

"Sorry?"

She spat. I wiped blood off my face. It speckled the surface of my lager and lime. "Do you mind?"

"Not so pretty now, is she?"

"Are you blaming me for... Listen," I said, "let's not waste time arguing. Selina's in a desperate..."

"She's my sweet daughter. I fed her with my own blood."

"You also murdered her girlfriend."

"So? I'm a mother, aren't I? With a mother's natural feelings. What else am I supposed to do?"

"Love her?"

"Of course I bloody love her. More than you ever will. Milksop mortal."

"Are you jealous?" I said, my temper rising.

"Jealous of you? *You*, incapable and riddled with fears like a worm-shot corpse?"

"You old blood bag!" I shouted.

"Ladies, ladies..." The Virgin Mary appeared between us, placing a restraining hand on Selina's mother's shoulder. The old woman had drawn back her upper lip, revealing two long and glistening canines. The Virgin bent and whispered something in her ear. On the next instant, to my surprise, the old bat vanished.

"Thank God," I said feelingly.

"You just got on her wrong side. She's very nice really."

"*Very nice?*"

"And wise. She's in my women's spirituality group."

Balancing a tray of empty beer mugs the Virgin Mary gazed at me, her glance sweet, loving and thoughtful. Courage flowed into me with that long look; I knew what I had to do.

I went home, walked into my bedroom where I had left Selina. She'd gone. There in her place, lying on the bed, was her mother.

Now I've seen dead people and dead was how she looked sunken eyelids   head tipped back   mouth a dark hole   I sat down beside her   not a heartbeat   I cupped her breast in my left hand, her shrunken old breast   I did that with my own mother's body, left alone with her open coffin in the visiting parlour   ancient gesture of reverence   I am flesh of your flesh   the difference being my mother's false teeth were taken out and her face sort of collapsed, but here the teeth were very much *in situ*   big white canines   all her strength in those teeth   silver hair like Selina's, but stringy and thin with bald patches   yellow skin cold, no blood in it   I am touching a dead thing   like a chicken before it goes in the oven   I asked my mother for blessing   mother, you gave me life   a life for a life   living with my mother was hell on earth but I made things right between us   I put my wrist to the old woman's mouth   take me   her eyes flickered open, her mouth bit down on me   clamp   oh my god   electric pain surges through my veins   what possessed me   some suicidal desire   love   she's got the main artery   like a baby greedily sucking   blood dribbles from the corners of her mouth   is this pain or exquisite pleasure   and she's changing   changing   silver hair   a pool of molten silver   face of a young girl

Selina   she raises herself above me   I've collapsed on the bed weak as a baby   she clasps my wrist to stop the blood spurting Joanna, she says   I didn't intend this should happen   not what I wanted   you understand don't you   Joanna, please don't die   darling, I reply faintly   self-control admirable   sparing my heart's blood   most unpleasant I'm sure it would have tasted   how are you feeling   I love you, she says, live forever   and sweet Virgin into your hands I commend my immortal soul.

The Secret of Sorrerby Rise

The Secret of Sorrerby Rise

A Tale of Mysterious Perils and Hazardous Adventure,
Leading to an Astonishing Discovery

I was born in the southern country of —shire, a place of gently swelling hills, mild summer skies, clear flowing rivers and trees gracefully waving in the warm caressing winds. A place "quiet as milk", as the country people say. My mother was a gentlewoman, cast off and abandoned by her rich hard-hearted relatives and yet bearing herself bravely in reduced and poverty-stricken circumstances. She took care to instil in me all the true female virtues – generosity, wisdom of mind and heart, love of all God's creatures and my own body. Above all, she encouraged my natural boldness and spirit of adventure. When I could scarce walk, she taught me my letters and so acquainted me at a tender age with the works of Mrs Radcliffe and Sir Horace Walpole.

My mother's beloved lifelong companion, whom I regarded with near-equal filial affection and respect, was one Miss Louisa Amersham. Sweet, loving spirit, may I ever continue to honour and bless thy memory! Louisa lingered on this earth only three days after my mother's death and they were buried together in one grave, in the little country churchyard, by the old grey church. Inseparable in death, as in life – their gravestone bears the following inscription:

Stranger, below this sod together rest
A matchless pair, and one another's Best.
Two female Friends, with but a single Heart,
Who met, were joined, and never now shall part.
Cruel Ignorance begrudged their Love reward.
Nature and Truth united to Applaud.

I now determined to seek my fortune in the world. For though I took pleasure in solitude and the healthy, well-regulated life of an independent countrywoman – quiet mornings devoted to study and philosophical reflection, the remainder of the day to hill-walking, sketching, cultivating my small vegetable garden, a spot of pugilism with the village lads, or fencing practice – yet this was not enough, could never be enough. My nature, ever warm and impulsive, demanded adventure, romance, passion. Destiny beckoned, and I must heed her call.

I decided to go north. Louisa's birthplace was in the northern country of —shire, and I had often heard her speak with enthusiasm of the beauty of the —shire moors and dales.

While still laying plans for my departure, I went one evening to scatter flowers and shed tears on my dear mothers' grave. Spring was then unfolding her brightest glories in field and woodland and by the murmuring brook, and I must linger to praise and exclaim; so the hours slipped away unnoticed and it was near midnight by the time I reached my destination.

The moon was full and sailing high among fast-blowing clouds;

trees cast flickering shadows over the white gravestones, like a multitude of ghosts gathering and fleeing at my approach. It was a romantic scene, worthy of a painter's hand – unluckily, I had left my sketchbook behind in the cottage.

As I stood in pensive silence, cursing my lack of forethought, I was arrested by an unexpected vision. A solitary figure was standing in a grassy clearing, beside my mothers' grave. From his bearing and attire he appeared a gentleman of means, and of advanced years. He had removed his hat and was standing with his white head bowed, in the attitude of one recently bereaved, and deeply shaken by grief. I drew closer, though hesitant to disturb his sorrowful meditations, but with the helpful intention of re-directing him to the right grave.

"Old Sir…" I began. With a start, he turned, and gazed upon me like one thunderstruck.

"Maria!" he uttered in a croak. "Maria, my dearest daughter! My long lost child!"

"Nay, Sir, you are mistaken. My name is not Maria, but Abigail. Maria was my mother's name. There she lies" – I pointed to the grave – "at rest, in the arms of Louisa, her beloved."

"You are her daughter, then?"

"I am."

"My dear child…" He touched my face, with a trembling hand. "You bear a remarkable resemblance to her. Those dark eyes – yet clear, and shining with the pure light of angelic goodness and unbending, courageous love. The sweetness of your expression withal – and your bearing, graceful and womanly. Heavenly angel!" he cried, falling to his knees. "You are indeed her child – Maria, my own daughter, whom to my eternal regret I banished from her parental home and deprived of her rightful inheritance. She was a young widow then, with an infant clinging to her breast, and her affectionate friendship with Louisa Amersham appeared to be transgressing all bounds of propriety. But oh, that I had stopped my ears to the scandalous rumours of spiteful gossip-mongers! My dearest treasure is forever lost to me. Too late now to beg her forgiveness, to offer recompense! She is dead, and by my hand, as surely as if I had killed her myself. Poverty destroyed her spirit – destitution brought her to an early grave..."

During all this time I had been attempting to persuade the poor old man to rise, and at last succeeded. I then represented to him earnestly, and with all the descriptive power at my command, what my mother's life had been – her happiness with Louisa, the rock she leaned upon in times of adversity, their love of Nature and the countryside, their busy, active and useful lives, their devoted friends. I described my mother's artistic achievements and many successfully executed commissions. I touched, with heartfelt gratitude, on her tender care of myself and concluding with the recollection of her steadfastness, courage and fortitude, even as the end drew near, I assured him that, whatever my mother's sufferings, she was incapable of bearing a grudge towards any fellow being, or feeling even the smallest trace of bitterness; he might therefore be confident of her complete and loving forgiveness.

By degrees, as I talked, I saw his anguish lose its initial sharpness, to be replaced by a more gentle melancholy. He stood watching while I scattered flowers from my basket o'er the grave. Then – "Dear daughter!" he exclaimed, "for may I so call you? Come with me to London, to my house in St James's Square. There, I can promise you a life of ease, security and good social standing. Solace my few remaining years and I will bequeath to you my entire fortune..."

I thanked him courteously for this offer, but instantly declined it. Inwardly, I shrank with horror at the prospect. Was my free, exultant soul to be thus bound in servitude, in the petty round of London masques, routs and balls, the paying of half-hour visits to Lady So-and-so and the Misses Such-and such, the leaving of cards and the making of social chit-chat, not to speak of *men* and their unwelcome attentions? No! I had better things to do with my life. Though scarce eighteen, I had formed some knowledge of my own nature. Above all things, I longed for a Friend, a true and lasting companion, such as I was unlikely ever to discover in that false and artificial world.

Upon further inquiry, I discovered that my grandfather was returning to the Great Capital that very night. He readily agreed to give me a lift to the nearest town, King's Ditchly, from whence I might catch a stagecoach to the North. Grasping this heaven-sent opportunity, I ran back to the cottage, packed my few modest belongings – principally my sketchbook, two changes of clothes, my sword and a treasured locket containing daguerreotypes of Louisa and my mother – then hastened to the village outskirts, where his carriage awaited me.

As we clattered through the narrow and twisting country lanes, overhung by the towering hedgerows, I was filled with excited apprehension and strove with difficulty to calm the wild beating of my heart. What might the future hold in store for me? Would I find adventure, happiness, love? In all events, I was determined against ever becoming a children's governess, that well-trodden path followed by so many other heroines before me.

At King's Ditchly, I descended from the carriage into a muddy cobbled street, and bade farewell to my grandfather, whose settled melancholy had by now dispersed like the dawn clouds, giving way to a more philosophical optimism – by morning, no doubt, he would be in fine spirits. Thus – transient and shallow – are men's feelings. He pressed upon me a small hamper of food and a bag of gold sovereigns. I thought it wisest to accept, having forgotten, in my haste, to bring any money with me.

There followed several days and nights of hard travelling, in broken-down, iron-seated stagecoaches, from town to town, between flea-ridden inns. This time is blurred and confused in my recollection, and I pass quickly over it – only to say that I was forced several times to repel coarse advances from *men*, and my opinion of the sex did not improve.

At length, weary and travel-stained, I reached the fringes of —shire and commanded a room in a modest but clean hostelry, run by an honest-seeming woman and her husband. Having dined excellently on roast parsnips and elderberry wine – eschewing the capons and sirloin of beef, in accordance with my strictest principles – I was shown by candlelight to a bedchamber above, where a cheerful fire was already lit. I bent over it with pleasure, holding my hands out to the leaping flames, and sinking on to a stool, I let the blissful warmth steal through my numbed and chilled limbs. (Accustomed from birth to the gentle and clement weather of the south of England, I had failed to anticipate the sterner northern climate, its bitter winds and harsh driving rains.)

Thus I remained, lost in reverie, until the fire was reduced to glowing coals and a clock chimed midnight in the hallway. Then of a sudden, I heard voices from the adjoining chamber, raised in altercation, and a woman's protest, followed by a scream. Without pausing to consider further, I grabbed my sword and rushed into the corridor. The next door was fast closed; I rattled the handle and shouted, but received no answer. Drawing back a little way, I hurtled with all possible force at the locked door, which burst open, precipitating me into the room.

Instantly, I found myself measuring swords with a man of middle age – thirty or so – in a curled and oiled wig, with cold grey eyes and a face marked by dissipation. Decidedly, a villain. Behind him shrank a young maiden of bewitching beauty, her blonde hair tumbling in disarray around her heaving bosom and her blue eyes filled with imploring terror.

After staring me a few moments, the villain slowly lowered his sword and returned it to the sheath, his lip curling in a disdainful half-smile. "Your pardon, Madam – from your manner of entrance, I took you for some common cut-throat or highwayman. I pray you, put up your sword – it becomes you ill, and I have no desire to murder a lady. No doubt you have misapprehended – this young woman is my niece, and I am accompanying her to London, to her father's house."

"He lies!" cried the girl energetically. "Lend no ear to these vile falsehoods! I am not this man's niece, nor ever will be – merely his third, fourth, or perchance even fifth cousin – and he has no natural authority, nor any rights over me. Were it not that I foolishly, without consideration... that I..." whereupon she burst into a shower of tears.

Her honour was clearly at stake, and mine also; for I took some pride in my swordsmanship, and was enraged by the man's insults. "Never fear!" I cried. "I am your sister, and will defend you to the death, if need be. Sir, I challenge you!" I thrust forward, ripping open his waistcoat. He flinched back in surprise, his eyes narrowing, and emitted a sound not unlike a hiss from between clenched teeth. We fought up and down the room, our swords flashing in the candlelight. I had the initial advantage of surprise, but was hampered by my dress; nevertheless, I had benefited from Louisa's instruction, and she was an excellent swordswoman. I was beginning to gain the upper hand, when he leapt behind a small table, kicking it towards me so that I stumbled over it – then, while I was still regaining my balance, he pinked me in the arm.

I fought on bravely with my left hand, and at length, with a cunning twist, sent his sword spinning across the room. "Mercy!" he cried, falling on his knees before me.

"You deserve none," I answered. "But nevertheless, I will spare your life – on condition that you first apologise to this lady, for attempting to force your unwelcome attentions upon her, and then leave this place instantly…"

With a sideways glance in her direction, he muttered something below his breath, the substance of which I construed as an apology, although the words were impossible to distinguish – then rose heavily and stumbled from the room. I kicked the door shut behind him.

Then turned.

Her eyes were heavenly blue, like summer skies, her skin so astonishingly fair and clear, it seemed almost transparent, her hair loosened of its bindings seemed to float around her like a shining golden mist. Her dress was of sprigged muslin, caught under her breasts with a ribbon, accentuating their soft fullness. Her mouth was like a cherry. Her nose was simple but charming. The speaking blood rose to her cheeks as I gazed upon her, imparting to them a delicate tinge, like a white rose flushed with the faintest hue of pink. A rose, I thought, just unfurled from the bud – with the fresh early morning dew not yet evaporated from her soft, velvety petals – fragrant, innocent, untouched. As I stood captured by admiration, she sighed and spoke. Her voice was clear and musical, yet low, and it thrilled me to the depths, to the very marrow, to my innermost soul. The precise words at first escaped me, so entranced was I, but at length I absorbed them.

"Now I suppose you, too, have fallen in love with me!" she exclaimed, in disconsolate, impatient tones. "Oh yes, don't trouble to deny it. I perceive the signs already – your moonstruck eyes and that foolish expression upon your face. Oh, why does this always..."

There came a loud commotion from the yard below – the snorting and alarmed neighing of horses, clattering on the cobbles, and a man's voice – that of my former opponent – uttering a string of voluble curses. "Damn you, Horace, let go! You'll ruin the creature's mouth! Here, take this!" – the sharp ringing of coins on stone.

My companion rushed to the window, and leaning out, cried "Stop him! Landlord, I charge you!" – then, as the sound of hooves faded, she uttered a despairing cry. "Oh God, he has stolen her! My dearest Belinda!"

She fell back, and threw herself on the bed, in a fury of impatient anguish.

"Who is Belinda?" I inquired.

"My horse, my sweet horse!"

"Are you very fond of her, then?"

"Oh, you have no conception! She means everything to me! She has all my heart! And now Roland – my wicked cousin – has ravished her from me!" And she burst once more into hysterical tears.

I made inarticulate sounds of sympathy, for her distress could not but move me, although personally I never had much of a fondness for horses. She raised her head and gazed at me, her eyes like drowned violets in a lake of milk. "I entreat you, go after him! Pursue him, the dastard! We must lose no time. Every second is precious – I am sure the landlord, honest Horace, would willingly lend you one of his horses..."

The room faded and grew dim, and my ears were filled with an immense roaring, like the sea or like wind sweeping over the hills. "Your pardon...at this moment I cannot..." I heard my voice coming as if from a long way off, and her dismayed exclamation – "Oh God, what is it? Your sleeve is soaked in blood! You are wounded!" Then I lost consciousness.

When I awoke, I was lying on a soft bed, near a shuttered window. I could see bright sunlight between the slats, and birds were singing musically outside. "Where am I?" was my first thought, then as memory flooded back, "and where is she? How long have I been lying here, unconscious, and what has transpired in the interval? Has that villain returned to abduct her, to force her against her will? Has he killed her? Alas the day!"

I struggled to rise, and at once sank back, overcome by dizziness. My arm was tightly bandaged, past the elbow, so I could scarcely move it; even my hand felt numb. Gazing round me, I saw my dress and undergarments laid over a chair. A clock ticked on the mantelpiece, above a fireplace heaped with grey ashes. A moment later, I heard a soft tread; the doorhandle turned and the innkeeper entered. A smile spread across her face on seeing me; approaching, she laid a cool hand on my forehead.

"How are you faring?" she inquired.

"Madam, I beseech you tell me, how long have I been lying here?"

"Three days and more. The fever has passed, thanks be."

"Where is the young lady who..."

"Whish, settle back now. She's long gone. She paid her account and rushed away like the wind in a great hurry – I doubt you'll ever catch up with her. But stay...now I recall, she left a letter for you..."

Stepping out of the room, she returned a moment later, holding a sealed document, tied up with ribands; this she extended towards me at arm's length and with a somewhat doubtful air. "Pray, fold back the shutters..." I implored. She did so, and the morning sunlight flooded in. I tore open the letter and eagerly devoured it, although the hand was near indecipherable: but at length I made out the following:

My dear Friend,

Forgive my discourtesy towards you: it was ill judged. The desperation of my predicament having raised my emotions to fever pitch, I can hardly be held responsible in the circumstances for what, in an unguarded moment, I may have ejaculated, although if it wounded your sensibilities I am sorry for it, but forsooth, let it pass, I am eternally grateful to you and should we ever meet again, I will endeavour to behave more kindly. I am now setting forth in search of Belinda, my beloved Horse, but first, to prove that I am not by nature heartless and insensible, let me relate to you the sorrowful story of my past life.

I was born the sole child of affectionate – too affectionate, alas! – parents. My father was a wealthy tradesman, who having achieved worldly success and prosperity early in his career was content to purchase an estate in the county of —shire and retire there. My mother willingly complied, being fatigued with the exigencies of London life, no longer in her first youth and somewhat depressed in spirits.

She and my father were both good people, and by all appearances seemed ideally suited: neither was bookish or had any odd freaks; in affairs of religion and politicks, their opinions exactly coincided. Yet they could not love one another. God knows by what miracle I came into the world at last, for certainly I never saw them embrace, or even touch. As the years passed, disinclination and coldness grew into a positive distaste for one another's company: no longer conversing, they kept separate rooms within the same house, my father in the east wing, my mother in the west. To hear either of them speak, you would think the other was no more than a distant, unfavoured relative.

Meanwhile I grew to girlhood, the helpless object of all their wasted, unspent affection; showered in equal measure by each with embraces, confidences and gifts. The more unhappy I became, it seemed, the greater their enthusiasm. I developed coughing and choking fits, which only increased their attentions. Their love was the very air I breathed, an element unsuited to my nature. Yet other children would crave such parental fondness. I felt as if I were drowning in a silver river, while those around me were dying of thirst...

But this, though bad enough, was not the limit of my sorrowful predicament. Scarce twelve years old, I was acknowledged universally as a Beauty, and receiving homage from all sides. Everybody I met seemed to fall in love with me – one gentleman, madly enamoured and attempting to scale the wall to my bedchamber, fell from a drainpipe and was killed; another, a melancholic, drowned himself; several were slain or horribly injured in duels; and so on. By my fifteenth year, I had received three times that many proposals of marriage, and suffered countless insults and indecent suggestions.

And not only from men! Nay, though innocently I had fled for protection and safety to the female sex, I soon discovered the naïvety of my conceptions. One governess after the other had to be dismissed without a character – cooks and kitchenmaids likewise. Even my aunt, a respectable married woman, made advances to me in the shrubbery, when she and I were sheltering from a rainstorm.

At last, my only place of refuge was the stables, where the groom and stable lad were happily enamoured only of one another; and there I first encountered my beloved Belinda. Horses are in every way preferable to human beings, I consider; their odour is sweeter, their intelligence more sensitive and refined; above all they are utterly indifferent to foolish aesthetic considerations. Belinda has no notion of my being beautiful or charming; she likes me because I feed her with apples and keep a light hand on the reins. I honour her judgement. She herself is a peculiarly ugly horse, but no words of mine can describe the sweetness and gaiety of her spirit. I cannot help but shed a tear, remembering. Forgive the brevity of this communication. I must depart instantly, in pursuit of Roland, my wicked cousin, for I feel sure he intends harm to Belinda.

Adieu – Marianne.

Having perused the foregoing epistle, I refolded it with a sigh, and fell back. "Well, there is no use in following her, even if I were capable of doing so. Marianne!" I breathed the lovely name aloud.

"Marianne!" echoed a mocking voice, behind me. I turned sharply, and saw to my utter astonishment and confusion, standing by my bedstead, a man! Though apparently a mere stripling, not more than eighteen, his manner was self-assured and easy – he seemed not in the least discomfited by my horrified gaze.

In stature he was of middle height, and slim. His hair was a light reddish brown, tied back with a riband and powdered. He wore a brown velvet coat, with darker lacing, and a cambric shirt, with a lace neck-cloth, falling in lavish ruffles. This modish style of dress gave him a somewhat foppish air, belied by the sword fastened neatly at his side. Also the swiftness of his movements – for before I knew it, he was gone from behind me and arranging himself comfortably on the broad window seat. His shapely legs were clad in white stockings and buckled shoes.

"Who is Marianne? Your sister, cousin, friend, mistress?"

A pang shot to my heart at the latter suggestion, but I bit my lip and strove to maintain a stony expression. "I wonder, Sir, that you should make it your business to inquire. Marianne is – a stranger to me – I encountered her but recently, and we parted not half an hour after meeting."

"Is that so?" His brow lifted and his gaze rested upon me, thoughtfully. "And will you – ah – encounter her again, in the foreseeable future?"

"How should I tell?" was my irritable rejoinder.

"I merely wondered."

"And I can only repeat, what business may it be of yours?"

"None at all – unless I should perchance take an interest in your affairs, and choose to involve myself therein."

"Pray desist from doing so. I would rather you left me – and my affairs – entirely alone." Unwisely, I made an abrupt movement, and winced.

"That arm is dressed very clumsily – no wonder it pains you. I understand something of physic... will you allow me...?" Before I could protest, he was at my side, untying the bandage. A faintness overcame me and my sight was dimmed for a moment: I heard his sharply indrawn breath on seeing the wound. "This must be cleaned, and the dressing renewed."

"No, I pray you..." I protested, weakly.

"My dear girl, you can trust my discretion, calm yourself."

"But I would rather have a woman..."

"I admire your discrimination. However, this is hardly the time to be debating the merits of the sexes..."

Those were the last words I heard; then I must have lapsed into unconsciousness, for when I next opened my eyes, he was gone.

I had slept deeply, and was filled with the sweetest sensation of peace, as if rocked gently and hushed in my own dear mother's arms. It was evening, and the moon cast down her luminous beams, suffusing my chamber with a soft radiance. Instantly I rose and walked to the window. My arm was loosely bound and no longer troubled me, although I was greatly weakened by the fever, and somewhat dazed by the rapid passing of recent events. "That extraordinary young man – who was he, I wonder? Did I dream of him, or does he exist in truth? Sure, I could never have imagined such a vision!" I smiled, remembering. "Despite his discourtesy, I liked him. He amused me and he was charming, unlike other men. I wonder if..."

I settled myself in the broad window enclosure, gazing out across the moonlit fields; and sighed deeply. "How ignorant I am! I understand nothing of man, or woman either. My own heart is an entire mystery to me. I have travelled far, yet for no good cause, and to no perceptible end – my destination becomes increasingly uncertain, ever retreating as I advance. Where shall I find true happiness? Am I wrong in settling my hopes on that elusive object – should I not rather strive to curb and restrain my perhaps too impulsive, too eager nature; by turning inwards, to rely ever more upon myself, establishing a surer foundation of self-knowledge and moral strength? Since I am now alone in the world, with none to care for me and nobody to love, and no reason to expect any change in this most painful predicament. Nay, since I fall in love so easily and on such slender acquaintance, it may be that I am incapable of forming any lasting attachment..."

Thus besieged by melancholy thoughts, and plunging ever deeper into self-induced despondency, I sat and wept; till of a sudden, some other influence, of relief, of comfort, seemed to enter my soul. I lifted my eyes and saw before me a vision – the face of a woman, old and wise – neither Louisa nor my mother, yet with something of each in her countenance.

"Arise, my daughter!" she exclaimed. "Forgo these bitter doubts and needless self-recriminations. Never doubt your capacity to love, and that you will receive abundant love in return. There is one who needs you and who is in peril of her life. You alone have the power to save her. Take courage, therefore, and struggle onwards..."

Her face shimmered and vanished. I was left alone, gazing at the blank and rounded full moon. Yet in spirit I was no longer alone – no longer despairing or wrought upon by the false phantoms of tremulous conscience. "So be it!" I exclaimed. "Great Mother of All, how can I choose but obey you, and follow rejoicing wherever you direct me?" And I passed several moments in silent thankfulness.

Pangs of hunger then assailed me, and recollecting that I had eaten nothing for nigh on three days, I dressed myself and hastened downstairs. I could discover little of sustenance in the larder, saving a number of dry biscuits, which I consumed with an eager appetite. Then, throwing a thick cloak over my shoulders, I drew the bolts of a side door, and stepped into the cobbled courtyard.

Dawn was then stretching her yellow fingers across the eastern horizon, and the joyous calling of birds rang clearly on the still air. A cock crew; a dog barked; deep sighs and impatient blowing noises came from the nearby stables. Taking a circuit of the building, I admired how the hillside rose up steeply and majestically behind; the little inn seeming to nestle in its depths, like a chick folded under her mother's wing. This situation would account, I reflected, for the extreme dampness of the structure, and the resultant gloomy and dank atmosphere of the lower rooms – "it be all thikky up the walls", as my countrymen would say.

Well, I had reached the North, and was already enchanted by it. Life moved here at an exhilarating pace; the very air seemed infused with passion and adventure; soon I hoped to make acquaintances less transient, or even friends. Though doubtless many of these —shire folk, as in other remote country places, would be dour and distrustful of strangers. On this point, I determined to interrogate my good hostess, whom by her quaint accents and turn of speech I judged a —shire woman born and bred. A moment later, I heard a stirring within the house and she emerged, throwing a bucket of slops into the courtyard.

She greeted me, though with a sober mien, and an air of heaviness – I hardly recognised my comforter of the previous morning. Without further preamble, she began, "You'll not have heard – and the tidings will hardly touch thee, being a foreigner..."

"What, I pray you?"

She drew closer to me, lowering her voice and casting a nervous glance back over her shoulder, as if wary of intruders. "A man was killed last night, crushed to death by a falling rock, as he was riding homewards, along by Carransfell..."

A chill struck to my heart, recalling my visitor, that young man of the lace ruffles and exquisite manners. I described him to my hostess, and she regarded me with astonishment. "Know you not who that was? 'Twas Lord Courtenay de L'Isle. From the concern he showed over thee, I felt sure he must be thy cousin or some other relative. No, 'twas not he, but —, a well-to-do farmer of this district..."

On further inquiry, I elicited the following sensational information: it appeared that this part of —shire was greatly infested with foot robbers; the roads being narrow and not seldom overhung by steep ledged outcrops of rock, these desperados would leap down from above on passing carriages; then, having disabled the coachmen and stripped those within of money and valuables, they would scatter and vanish into the surrounding hills.

However, the terrain was in general bare and bleak, offering few hiding places; or it turned quickly from rocky crags to open moorland. To forestall pursuers, the robbers had lately adopted a most cruel and dastardly practice. One of their number would remain above, overlooking the scene, and on a pre-arranged signal, would send rocks of a massive size tumbling and bouncing down the hillside. These would oftentimes hurt or kill innocent travellers, or else fright the horses, causing them to bolt, or set off a landslide, crushing all below and blocking the road for many days hence.

As my hostess was talking the sun rose clear of the eastern horizon, bathing the fields in dewy light. It was a scene of awesome beauty, and moved me deeply; yet admiration mingled strangely in my heart with sensations of pity and horror, resultant on my landlady's revelations. "This beautiful landscape, which appears with the freshness and untouched glory of Eden, is yet tainted by human evil," I reflected. "Nature nurses a viper in her bosom, a wilful and vicious son at her breast. Oh, that Man could be wiped from this earth!"

My thoughts reverted to Marianne – had she succeeded in overtaking that odious brute, Roland, and recapturing Belinda, without further hazard or mischance? Surely the villain would let slip no opportunity to insult her afresh – and she defenceless, unprotected... Meanwhile, my hostess was still talking, being clearly of a voluble disposition, and before long, to my great astonishment, began to expound on this very subject. She informed me that Marianne was now safe, that – wonder of wonders! – Lord de L'Isle himself had pursued Roland and recaptured Belinda, giving Roland a large sum of money in exchange – further, that Marianne was Lord de L'Isle's ward, and that he owned most of the land thereabouts. This was strange indeed!

"But is not Lord de L'Isle very young?" I ventured. "If he is the gentleman who recently accosted me in my bedchamber – he seemed in the very bloom of youth, the lightest of down upon his cheek..."

"Nay – he looks young, I grant ye, but he is thirty. His parents died when he was just come of age, bequeathing him all their wealth, and a great castle on Sorrerby Rise; you may just glimpse its turrets, beyond that wood... He travels much abroad, but in the intervals of his journeying, he has made great improvements to the estate and the village – building cottages for the poor and a new schoolhouse. Blessings on him! He is loved by all hereabouts, and deservedly so. 'Tis our dearest wish that he should marry, and produce an heir – otherwise, should he by some sad accident chance to die, the estate would fall by default to that villainous cousin of his, that Mr Roland Hooker Waller" – my hostess pronounced this name with a fine disdain.

"Mr Hooker Waller – the gentleman I crossed swords with, three nights past?"

"Aye, the very same, excepting he's no gentleman. Sewer rat would be a more fitting description, for he's most vicious and corrupt – even to speak of him, it brings the bile swimming in my throat" – in eloquent proof of which, she spat on the cobbles.

"Is Mr Hooker Waller then universally disliked?"

"Aye, in these parts. He only hangs around here to cause mischief – otherwise he's mostly in London, gambling and frittering away his fortune – I should rather say, my Lord's fortune."

"How!" I exclaimed. "Is Lord de L'Isle then so blind to his cousin's faults – so easily deluded by him – so readily imposed upon? Does he bestow money freely upon this unworthy object – thus condoning, by implication, Mr Hooker Waller's debauched and vicious lifestyle?"

"I fear 'tis so," she replied. "Nothing is more mysterious, for Lord de L'Isle has as sharp and good a wit as any man, yet in this matter he appears befuddled and inconstant. Mr Hooker Waller comes and goes as he pleases, partaking frequently of Lord de L'Isle's hospitality – my lord keeps a fine cellar and the covers are laid each night, as befits his rank..."

She continued talking thus, digressing proudly on the subject of my lord's wealth, nobility, condescension, and so on, but I heard no more; my head was in a whirl of new conceptions. So Mr Hooker Waller was a regular guest at the Castle – at Marianne's place of residence – and invited, nay even welcomed there by her so-called guardian, her supposed protector! What could be the meaning of this? Instantly I was filled with burning resolution – I must seek out Marianne and if possible rescue her from the dread Castle, or at least offer her my service and protection – my heart, my sword, my life!

With this confirmed intent, I set out later that day, by foot, across the fields, and following the bank of a pleasant meandering river, soon arrived at the western boundary of Lord de L'Isle's estate. Here I paused – for the day was exceeding hot – to splash my face and dabble my feet in the clear running water. Impatient with constriction, I untied my bonnet and loosened my hair, so it tumbled free. Now truly I felt a daughter of Nature – like to some river naiad, or a dryad of the nearby woods. Sadly tanned and freckled, my hands roughened by country labour, I possessed nothing of Marianne's fair and ethereal beauty – yet my own body pleased me well enough. Sure, I would never wish to be a boy!

It was midday, and the sun having attained her zenith, the heat and glare were near insupportable. Instead of approaching the main gate of the Castle, therefore, I decided to walk through the woods, trusting to my luck and sense of direction, and hoping not to fall into any concealed mantraps. The beechwood was cool, well shaded and pleasant, though unexpectedly deep; an hour or so later, I was completely lost, and doubted my chances of emerging before nightfall.

It was then I heard voices nearby; familiar voices; one low and well modulated, the other raised in sneering deprecation. Lord de L'Isle and Mr Hooker Waller! I crept forward, and before long found myself on the edge of a wide clearing.

The greensward was closely mown, and marble statues were disposed here and there, representations of goddesses and the heroines of classical mythology. In the centre stood Lord de L'Isle, a slim and upright figure, now dressed in satin small clothes and a coat of excellent tailoring, fitting tightly across the shoulders. As I perceived him, my heart seemed to miss a beat, or several, and my breath quickened, yet recollecting the brevity of our connection and the kindness he had hitherto shown me, I strove to calm myself. Surely I had no reason to fear the man – if I were discovered, it was unlikely he would do me any harm, or even reprove me for trespassing on his land. Mr Hooker Waller, at a few yards' distance, lounged indolently against a statue of Atalanta, smoking a cheroot.

"My dear cousin, pray cease to trouble yourself thus needlessly. I meant no harm to the girl, nor to that – one may scarce call it a horse – to that animal. I beg you will forget the whole disastrous episode – believe me, it is of very little significance."

"Not to you, perhaps," Lord de L'Isle replied, evenly. "But you may recollect, Roland, that Marianne is my ward. Her parents being dead, I am now entrusted with her safe keeping – a duty which, believe me, I take seriously."

"But how delightful for you. Mixing duty with pleasure, so to speak."

"My task has so far proved the very opposite of delightful, or pleasurable. As you are well aware – and mainly due to your own interference…"

"My dear sweet coz, how can this be? I strive only to please you, in all things."

"You would please me best by keeping your distance – by continuing to reside in London, as I think we agreed, and confining yourself to twice-yearly visits."

"Ah yes, but then the air here is so invigorating, the prospects so charming, and despite having a monthly income – your most generous settlement, dear coz – somehow I find myself continually short of money."

"Due to foolish extravagance."

"Possibly." Mr Hooker Waller finished his cheroot and threw it on the ground, grinding it with his heel.

"At all events, let me entreat you…"

"Let us postpone your so-elegant entreaties to some future time; as you are aware, I dislike being lectured" – he took out a pocket watch – "and I am engaged to be in London tomorrow night, so if you will excuse me" – and sweeping a low, mocking bow, he withdrew. I now perceived that the clearing formed the central meeting place of three wide and majestic avenues. Mr Hooker Waller sauntered away down the furthest of these, which I assumed led back to the house.

Left alone, Lord de L'Isle exhibited every sign of irritable exhaustion and despondency. He struck his forehead, and aimed several kicks at a statue of Venus reclining at her toilet; then sinking into a conveniently placed bench, of curious and ornate design, he rested his head despairingly in both hands, and moaned aloud.

It was scarcely possible to remain any longer in concealment. I could not thus stand by as witness to the distress and suffering of a fellow human being, without seeking in some way to alleviate it; and besides, I owed this particular gentleman a debt of kindness; so I walked forward. He remained unconscious of my presence till I was but a yard away; then a twig cracked, and he looked up in surprise. Recognition dawned in his eyes, followed by another expression, of glad interest.

"If I am disturbing you, my Lord, I crave your pardon, but I... I..." My voice faltered and died.

"You are not," he replied, gently. "Pray sit down – I am happy to see you again, even at such a time as this. How much did you overhear of what just passed?"

"Hardly anything." I sat down beside him, feeling confused and somewhat shy. He was so elegant! – unlike anybody I had ever known. His well-manicured nails and long fingers, his lightly powdered hair, the intricate fall of his necktie – all bespoke a gentleman of high breeding. Even his skin seemed to waft a faint perfume... How could *I* have anything in common with someone so infinitely civilised?

"Marianne is then your ward?" I ventured.

"Yes – and I owe you an apology, for my former behaviour. I was not quite open with you – for you see, I suspected you of being involved in my cousin's conspiracy."

"How!" I exclaimed in astonishment. "Me, conspire with Mr Hooker Waller to abduct your ward?"

"Believe me, where Marianne is concerned, anything is possible – she attracts abductors, lovers, what you will, as a honey pot attracts flies. And do you then deny... did you never feel..." His eyes held mine, and I felt the blood rise to my cheeks. "Never mind," he said, quickly. "I will not question you."

We sat for some while in silence. I perceived with dismay the full awkwardness of my position – for had it not indeed been my professed object in coming here to abduct Marianne, in the guise of a rescuer and supposedly in her interests? The arrows of self-accusation struck to my heart and remained there, quivering; I was o'erspread with shame's mantle.

My companion meanwhile had recommenced speaking, thanking me with sincerity for my protection of Marianne, and regretting my wound. Observing my confusion, he let the subject lapse and began instead to ply me with questions concerning my past life – where was my birthplace and what my parentage? I replied at first with hesitancy, but gradually gaining confidence, told him something of my mother and of Louisa.

He regarded me with wonder. "And is it so?" he cried at last. "Did these two women spend their lives together in happy and enduring love, faithful even unto the grave? And were these your parents?"

"My father died when I was a babe," I replied. "Louisa was my loving guardian, friend, sister and teacher; to my mother, all these and more, far more. They were happy indeed – and as for me, I should count myself fortunate to find a Friend of one tenth Louisa's worth."

"I believe you," he returned, warmly "and I wish that I had known your stepmother, your guardian – she sounds a remarkable woman and an example to her Sex. I should have valued her acquaintance."

"But she would scarcely have valued yours, for she greatly mistrusted and despised all *men*." I spoke without thinking, and instantly regretting my words, wished that I had stayed silent – yet indeed, I had spoken nothing but truth.

He smiled faintly. "And did she so? I have known other Ladies of that persuasion – friends of mine, whose judgement I approve entirely. Yet these Ladies, though despising my Sex in general, have made an exception for me."

"Why so?"

"I cannot say. You will have to ask them. As it happens, they will be arriving here tonight, bringing a large party from London – they find my house a convenient place for dances and soirées. I could procure you an invitation, if you are willing to stay. I believe it is a coming-out ball."

While he was speaking, the sky had darkened rapidly, and soon huge drops of rain were falling here and there, in certain promise of a storm. We moved quickly to shelter, and taking my hand, he led me after him through the woods, until soon we came to a small roofed pavilion or summer-house, at a vantage point above the landscape.

It was a most glorious scene. From where we stood, the smooth green hillside swept down unhindered to a vast lake, which curved in serpentine fashion into the distance, giving the illusion of a winding river. In more clement, bright weather, I could imagine how the lake surface would glitter with a thousand sparkling lights; but now overhung by tumultuous grey clouds, it conveyed an awesome and sombre majesty. At some distance, I could see a foaming Cascade; near to it, the ruins of an Abbey; and on a far hillside, the entrance to what must be a network of underground Caves. Above all, I admired how clumps of trees stood here and there, most pleasing in their arrangement and drawing the eye towards distant prospects. The entire scene possessed all the splendour of an Italian painting; an effect unspoilt by the driving rain, now moving in sheets across the land.

"And did Nature do all this?" I exclaimed.

"She did little – although all was done in her Name," replied Lord de L'Isle. "The main part was contrived by Alice Brown, also known as Possibility Brown, a landscaper of consummate genius, though small fame – her brother takes all the credit for her work.

"And there is my house" – he pointed to the right. At half a mile's distance against the grey sky I saw a huge castle with crenellated battlements, its every window blazing with light. A number of carriages were visible, drawn up outside the main gates.

"My guests have arrived," he added. A smile crossed his lips, yet in his eyes lingered an indefinable expression of sadness. Watching him, I realised that, despite his noble birth, his great wealth and fashionable friends, Lord de L'Isle was yet unhappy – even lonely. For a moment I glimpsed his true self, behind the mask. I wished to speak, yet dared not – and the next instant, he turned towards me.

As our eyes met, my heart seemed to dissolve into liquid silver, and for a moment I was near fainting. I could no longer deceive myself – I was stricken with dismay – surely it could not be that I loved a Man! Nothing in my upbringing had prepared me for such a horrible eventuality – it ran contrary to all my former inclinations and against all my most fervently held principles.

Turning aside, I strove to regulate my emotions and compose my features – happily, it was still raining, and my distress concealed, so I hoped, by the more general atmospheric turmoil.

At that moment, I heard the calling of a sweetly familiar voice, and Marianne appeared over the hill, in company with another Female – both were clad in voluminous riding capes, ample protection against the Elements. Marianne was leading a horse, whom by the simple plainness of her countenance and her cross-eyed squint, I assumed to be Belinda.

Marianne made exclamations of surprised pleasure on catching sight of me and saluted me on both cheeks, in sisterly fashion; I gladly returned the embrace. Meanwhile, the other female was shaking hands with Lord de L'Isle. She was a large woman, and in her manner and bearing, reminded me somewhat of Louisa, for though she wore no ornaments and was far from the ideal of female beauty – her greying hair was bound back severely, her nose a forbidding beak – yet she was obviously of high birth and accustomed to command. Soon she accosted me with a friendly air, made inquiry of my name and demanded an account of my past life and present journey; I answered her honestly, as seemed best.

While I was speaking, she and Lord de L'Isle exchanged several glances; and I thought he looked steadily at me, though I could not, for fear, meet his gaze.

"My dear," she said at length, "I am Melissa Cheverel. I knew your stepmother, Louisa, in her youth, and loved her well – indeed I may say that I owe everything to her good offices, for she encouraged and by example aided my Conversion, leading me to escape from the miserable constrictions of family and stultifying respectability. Through her I first encountered the author and foundation of all my present happiness, Amaryllis, to whom I will introduce you this evening. I assume you are coming to the Ball?"

I knew not how to reply, for though her kindness touched me and I was pleased to make her acquaintance, yet I was hardly in a mood for festivity. Besides, what would this great Lady think of me, when her clear gaze penetrated, as it surely would, the turmoil of my heart – when she discovered my perverted affection for Lord de L'Isle, which I could hardly yet admit even to myself? Surely she would turn from me in revolted scorn?

The rain lessening, our party began to descend the hillside. Belinda's pace was uneven, as she would often pause to crop the fresh verdure; so the others drew ahead, while Marianne, taking my arm, proceeded to discourse with animation on the superior wisdom of Animals. I attended with a heavy heart.

"Oh!" she exclaimed "that human beings would only cultivate Natural Understanding – taking our example from such as my dear Horse. Our true needs are indeed very few and easily satisfied – principally for shelter and sustenance. Passionate love is a disorder of the natural emotions, resulting oftentimes in madness, and certainly antagonistic to Right Living. I am a subscriber to the New Philosophy of Mrs M. Humphry Allenby – if you are curious, I will gladly lend you her two most recent publications, the *Rediscovery of Happiness* and the *Return to Innocence*. Mrs Allenby's character is wholly admirable, and her writings would persuade even the..."

With a sudden access of spleen, I interrupted her. "No doubt – but Marianne, whatever the extraordinary virtues of Mrs M. Humphry Allenby – whatever higher state this lady may happily have attained – *you* are still susceptible to passionate error; for but a few days past, I seem to recall, you consented foolishly to elope with Mr Hooker Waller."

"No, indeed! You are wholly mistaken on that score. Roland cunningly deluded me – I believed his intentions to be entirely honourable."

"How! You thought he would offer marriage?"

"No – but he promised to accompany me to the horse fair at Mickleton Cross, which I had a great desire to see. Pray do not berate me – indeed, I deeply regret my naïvety on that occasion, especially as my dear guardian was forced to pay for it."

Again we paused, for Belinda to savour an especially nourishing piece of vegetation. Lord de L'Isle and Miss Cheverel were now lost to view, having passed through the Castle gates.

But why, I wondered, should Lord de L'Isle have given money to Mr Hooker Waller – wherefore such craven behaviour towards a traitorous and despicable villain? Was this not strange? I expressed my bewilderment to Marianne, and she flushed.

"My guardian has a – a secret, which I am not at liberty to reveal. It explains All – and yet for his own safety, it must remain closely guarded. Perhaps if you ask him – I note he has a fondness for you..."

My heart gave a lurch. A fondness! Yes, he was fond of me – no more than fond. As for love – no. Perhaps he loved Marianne – or perhaps Mr Hooker Waller! Yes, that was surely the explanation: Mr Hooker Waller had spurned Lord de L'Isle's advances and was now blackmailing him, threatening to reveal his secret passion to the world! My mind moved with a marvellous rapidity, building conjecture upon conjecture. Thus engaged, to the exclusion of all else, I took absent-minded leave of Marianne in the stable courtyard and wandered into the great entrance hall of the Castle.

All around was bustle and movement – here a chambermaid scurried past carrying a pile of bed linen, and another with silver branched candlesticks; there two cooks, in animated discussion; and here a deputation of gardeners, bringing baskets of earthy vegetables and orchard fruits. All were women – a peculiarity that failed to strike me at the time, for I was admiring the vastness of the hall, with its flagstoned floor and huge pillars soaring to a fan-vaulted ceiling.

The housekeeper came forward, seemingly unsurprised by my arrival, and welcomed me kindly, introducing herself as Mrs Weston. She led me up a broad staircase and along a corridor hung with portraits; then, selecting a key from the bundle at her waist, she unlocked a door and opened it.

On entering the chamber, I exclaimed aloud with delight; for besides being nobly furnished, with a majestic four poster bed and ornately framed pictures and looking glasses on the walls, it was decked throughout with the most beautiful flowers. They were principally roses – roses of the deepest red and the purest white, and of heavenly scent. As I stood captivated, several chambermaids entered, carrying jugs of steaming hot water, which they poured into a tub, standing on feet fashioned like animal paws.

Mrs Weston turned to me. "My Lord gave instructions, Miss, that you would need dry stockings and shoes and a gown for tonight's ball. Everything is provided here, as you will find…" She unlocked the closet and left it a little ajar, then curtseyed and withdrew.

All was peaceful, save for occasional sounds of laughter, and women's voices below the windows: Lord de L'Isle's guests, I presumed, now taking exercise in the gardens, following the passing of the storm. Glancing down, I saw my garments were sodden with rain and liberally splashed with mud. I undid my gown and stepped out of it; then thought it best to uncover my long-forgotten wound, which proved to be near healed.

Curious to view my reflection, I walked forward to the nearest glass; and to my surprise, found that I looked almost beautiful. My eyes, darker and more open, my parted lips, the burning summer in my cheeks – all betrayed what I would fain conceal.

In the ensuing silence, I heard a rose drop her velvet petals, one by one; some fell on the carpet, and others into my bath water, where they floated and idly drifted.

I bathed with pleasure, and emerged from the water in good spirits.

Opening the closet, I found a dress of yellow silk and brocade, heavy and richly patterned, with a hooped petticoat and another of silver lace. Ranged on a shelf below were a great many shoes – I liked best a pair of yellow satin, which happily fitted me exactly. Rejecting a fan of painted chicken skin with ivory sticks, I picked another of gilded paper.

The day was fading and a maid entered carrying a taper, to light the candles in my room. She was very young and herself appeared surrounded by a soft radiance of golden light – it seemed she might have kindled the candles just with her fingertips. She stayed to help me with my hair, and from time to time gave a gentle sigh.

"What ails you?" I demanded. She made no answer, but her eyes, meeting mine in the glass, told all. Love is indeed the finest melancholy, spilling over in sighs and tears. "Will you meet her tonight?" I asked.

She nodded. "But first I must light all the candles, and help the ladies to dress..."

I took the comb from her hand and pushed her towards the door. "Go now," I said. "Leave your taper; I shall light the candles. The ladies can dress themselves, I dare say."

Instruments were being tuned below and would occasionally break into a waltz or quadrille. I felt a growing excitement. This would be my first ball! – and perhaps if I drank enough negus or ratafie, I might put Lord de L'Isle from my thoughts and find my affections turning towards a more suitable object.

I went down the corridor, knocking and entering at every door. Some of the bedchambers were empty; in others I encountered a lady at her toilet, or several of them together, laughing and talking. I received some curious glances, but lit the candles and was gone before any could question me.

Having crossed the stairwell, I came to an oaken door of imposing dimensions. I tried the handle; it opened easily and I entered carrying my taper before me.

The room was huge and made sombre by the deepening dusk. I could descry a bay window at the far end, and bookcases lining the two long walls and reaching to the ceiling – itself an impressive specimen of ornate plasterwork. I walked forward incautiously, prompted by my desire to examine the books; nearest were a number of bound calfskin volumes of Shakespeare's plays and the collected works of Mr Pope; but I got no further, for a shadowy figure moved with heart-stopping suddenness from an alcove and strong fingers closed around my wrist. I gasped for fright and nearly dropped the taper – but he took it from me in time. It was Lord de L'Isle!

Keeping his eyes steady upon mine, he moved back a pace; then turned to light a branch of candles, standing in a niche. Our shadows danced and stretched up to the ceiling.

He was dressed in grey satin with old lace at his wrists and throat, a dress sword fastened by his side, and broad diamond buckles on his shoes.

"Did you hope to avoid me?" he said, lightly.

"I... I... no," I stammered. "I had no such desire – I am honoured to be your guest."

"Yet your expression indicates a certain displeasure. Pray tell me, have I disgusted you in any way – or insulted you?"

"No..."

"Then why...?"

The blood rose to my face in a burning tide. My wrist still ached sorely from his clasp and I rubbed at it with a sense of grievance – it would very likely bruise. In sudden anger, I exclaimed, "I need not tell you my thoughts – you have no right to interrogate me. You keep your own secrets – then let me keep mine!"

A window was opened beneath. Sweet strains of music floated out on the evening air, and then a woman's voice singing:

Whoe'er she be
That not impossible She
That shall command my heart and me;

Where'er she lie,
Lock'd up from mortal eye
In shady leaves of destiny:

– Meet you her, my wishes
Bespeak her to my blisses,
And be ye call'd, my absent kisses.

Feeling a little giddy headed, I sank into the window seat. "Have you eaten?" he enquired.

"Not since this morning..."

"There is a cold collation laid out below – but if we are to exchange heart's confidences, it had best not be in a crowded ballroom. Besides, your descent is eagerly awaited – I would scarce have you to myself a moment. Let me order a tray to be brought up." He tugged the bellpull.

"By the way, you know it is a masked ball this evening. I have always been greatly interested in masks. When I was young, I spent a year in Venice, where the mask-makers ply their trade, by the Bridge of Sighs. Of these the most famous was Bartolomeo de San Servino, who had begun his career by casting the death masks of great noblemen and poets. His masks were so like real faces, you would believe they smiled sometimes, or grew melancholy. I saw a mask he made of the moon, that was said to confer immortality upon its owner: but you would have to accustom yourself to waxing and waning. One young married lady of my acquaintance sold her beautiful pearl ring and her emerald brooch to buy his mask of a female wolf. She was advised not to wear this until after her confinement was past, but the Carnevale falling in her sixth month, she could not resist – the results were exactly as predicted. Her husband ordered the child to be drowned.

"As for me, I was twenty-one, my parents had just died, I was unable to sleep at nights. When I entered the mask shop, Bartolomeo himself came forward to the counter: he looked not more than twenty, though I believe in that year he was 102. He refused to serve me, informing me that it was not advisable to place one mask on top of another. 'That you wear,' he said, pointing in my face, 'is already in a way to killing you.'

"In the next week, made bold by terror, I revealed my secret to a number of friends; then I felt the mask loosen its grip; I gained a little breathing space. Otherwise, I do believe it would have suffocated me. For you see, it is one of those dead men's faces. I had a twin brother and he was the heir to my parents' estate; when we were ten years old and my mother past childbearing age, he died. Anxious to secure the succession – for the estate, like most, was entailed in favour of a male heir – they determined that *I* should be a boy – that I should be, in effect, my brother. So they gave it out, 'twas the girl that died.

"And now, since I have told you my secret, can you trust me with yours?"

Mrs Weston had answered the bell, and brought us a number of little dishes on a tray, and gone away again, before I was anywhere near speaking.

"And Mr Hooker Waller?" I managed at last. "Is he aware of – of what you have just told me?"

"If he were, the whole of Society would also know it within a day or two, and Roland would be installed in his rightful place, as Master of this estate. He would be Lord de L'Isle – and I, plain Cordelia Beaufort. He senses his power over me, none the less, and makes use of it. I expect he will find out eventually – then I shall be forced to flee the country and live abroad – the estate will go to rack and ruin under his ownership, for he would care naught, either for the land or for its people. You may well think me an unsuitable protector for Marianne – possessing a borrowed past and no future, living ever in the uncertain present – but at least I provide a home for her. Her parents entrusted her to me, knowing all. If you love her indeed, I give you leave to hazard your suit, though you have not much chance of success, I warn you... others have tried..."

I stood up, though doubting the strength of my legs, but apprehending that I must speak now, seizing the opportune moment, and disperse all lingering clouds of doubt and illusion. "I would make a poor suitor in truth, for my heart is already given away. I love you, Cordelia! – and consequent upon your most welcome revelation, my Will and my Reason now join with my Heart, in preferring you above all others. If you will not have me, I must... I must..." I was meaning to say, I must depart, and glanced uncertainly towards the door, but at that instant, she seized me in her arms and kissed me!

Oh! – the joy that flooded my heart! – I had never imagined, never allowed myself to conceive such happiness! It seemed natural and easy to return her embraces – though having the advantage of me in height and strength, she pressed me to her so hard I could scarce breathe and was soon forced to entreat her for a moment's respite. As she released me, I saw that her eyes were shining and her cheeks flushed – all bitterness and cynicism vanished from her countenance – no longer the sad young man, but a woman of great beauty and noble demeanour. Our lips met again, this time with tender hesitancy.

"Oh Abby," she breathed, "stay with me, be mine – I will love you for ever!" Taking my hand, she covered it with kisses.

"Yes dearest, for a lifetime and more. We must never again be parted, I could not endure it. As to where we live," I added, "it hardly matters – this Castle is wholly delightful, but indeed I would welcome the opportunity of foreign travel."

Our conversation continued a good while longer, mixed with a thousand caresses and sweet endearments, which having pity on my reader, I forbear to describe. At eleven o'clock, with exceeding reluctance, we descended to the ballroom, where Melissa welcomed us with composure and the merest flicker of a raised eyebrow. I was introduced to stately Amaryllis, Duchess of —, and a great number of other ladies, including several of the old nobility, others of scholarly renown or possessed of great artistic genius, and many fresh in the bloom and gaiety of youth. Having never before seen ladies dancing together, or paying such open tribute of sisterly kindness and affection, I revelled in the Spectacle; it recalled to me the poet's words:

There all the happy souls that ever were,
Shall meet with gladness in one theatre;
And each shall know, there, one another's face,
By beatific virtue of the place...

The central embellishment of the long refreshment table was an Ice Bowl, filled with chopped fruits; a device of marvellous conception and cunning execution; for though composed of frozen water it did not melt, only its frosty surface after several hours turned clear and glistened; and sweet pea flowers hung suspended therein, as if growing in air. This appeared to me an emblem of the heart: she who desires love must be content to wait in patience for her reward; break the bowl before it melts and you would tear and destroy the flowers – and so on.

I had almost forgot to say, Mr Hooker Waller came to a violent end – for having stayed late and drunk deep that night in the village tavern, and falling in with a pack of dastardly ruffians, and attempting in their company to rob a gentleman's carriage, he was first shot and then crushed by a rock. So all ends happily.

More new fiction from Diva Books

The Ropemaker's Daughter
Virginia Smith

A gripping debut about truth, lies and pretenders

Rebecca habitually questions the people she meets and steals the
stories they tell her, claiming them for her own. But then she meets a
man whose story is already familiar, a man who says he knows her.
The real Adam threw himself off a cliff ten months earlier – so who is
this imposter, and what does he want? Enter Paige, who wants to help
Rebecca discover the truth about herself, about Adam – and about love
between women. But even she may not be what she seems.

**"I read it in one sitting. I defy you to do otherwise"
Manda Scott (author of *No Good Deed*)**

**"Packed with juicy red herrings and slick plot twists... keeps you
guessing until the end" Rainbow Network**

**"Lovers of Barbara Vine will adore Smith's plotting... takes you
on a fantastic ride" Gay.com.uk**

"Gripping" *3 Sixty*

RRP £8.99 ISBN 1-873741-70-7

Maddie and Anna's Big Picture
Jane Marlow

A witty look at the messy 'big picture' of modern relationships

Rents in London are soaring and for Anna, a City lawyer with an eye for figures, buying a flat together has never made more sense. But for her girlfriend Maddie, the transition from idealistic twenty-something artist to thirty-something home-owner is a little more problematic. Wishful thinking doesn't match reality and monogamy is proving quite a challenge.

If only they could be more like their friends: Kat doesn't want to settle down, Julia and Ed don't need to live together, and Andy just likes a good time...

"A delicate, witty picture of modern life, containing some gorgeous, classic observations on life. I loved it because it just feels real" Russell T Davies, creator of *Queer As Folk*

"A version of love and lust that is gratifyingly honest in its intricacies, thoughtful in its language – *A Midsummer Night's Dream* with career, finances and property as the meddling fairies" Stella Duffy

RRP £8.99 ISBN 1-873741-71-5

How to order your new Diva Books

Diva Books are available from bookshops including Silver Moon at Foyles and Libertas! or direct from Diva's mail order service:
www.divamag.co.uk or freephone 0800 45 45 66
(international: +44 20 8340 8644).

When ordering direct, please add P&P (single item £1.75, two or more £3.45, all overseas £5) and quote the following codes:
The Ropemaker's Daughter ROP707,
Maddie & Anna's Big Picture MAD715, Absent Kisses ABS782